One Hundred Days

Martin exchanged his cap for a helmet, pulled on his greatcoat and went into the squalling rain. The first mile or so was easy going on good roads, but the further he went the worse it got. Duckboards crossed a sea of mud with shell craters forming little lakes all over the place. Horses had bogged in the mud attempting to get guns and ammunition into place, and were shot when they could travel no further. A small number of gunners attempted to fire their weapons while others worked at stopping their guns from sinking into the ooze on each recoil. The duckboards came to an end, shelled to pieces, and Martin took to the mud and sank half-way to his knees. He struggled onwards one step at a time and knew what the problem was. The men couldn't advance on such ground. On the right stretcher bearers carried a casualty with great difficulty, some up to their waists in mud. Martin slowed his pace, probing the ground for firmness before the next step. That way he wouldn't sink too deep. Indeed he wondered if any men had sunk much too deep, and were not shot or shelled but just trapped in the mud. Horses, carts, artillery, tanks lay scattered about; not shelled but bogged and abandoned. And for what it was worth the rain stopped. Martin pressed onwards because he said he would do so, but he wondered how he could find out what was going on. He reached the reserve trenches, kept his head low because he was tall, and pressed on along the duckboards. Closer and closer to the front trench with ladders still in place. On his right was a single soldier sitting with his back against the breastwork of the support trench while smoking a cigarette. He didn't look too good. "Can I help you?" Martin asked, getting to his knees.

"My leg...," the soldier said wincing in pain.

Martin glanced down, but the mud on the soldier's uniform hid any injuries. "I'm sure the stretcher bearers will be here soon. My name's Martin."

"I'm Jack."

"What happened out there Jack?"

"It was hopeless. We had little artillery, and the shells they fired sank into the mud without exploding. Our machine guns wouldn't work in the mud, we struggled to get through the mud, some even drowned, but the Hun pillboxes were undamaged and caused bloody slaughter. So many mates...."

"I'm sorry to hear about your mates." Martin looked around. "Can you walk if I help you?"

"I made it this far on my own so I might be able to."

Martin grabbed under Jack's muddy shoulders and lifted him, and with Jack using Martin as a support and his rifle as a crutch, they were able to return along the communication trench. "Those bloody generals...," Jack muttered.

"Don't blame all the generals Jack. There are some who didn't want this to go ahead."

"Our lot I suppose."

Martin didn't say a word. They struggled on and eventually a stretcher party approached. "Sir," one of the bearers said.

"I'm not a sir I'm Martin. You look after this man."

"We will."

Martin left them and headed out of the trench complex and west towards Ypres, to Menin gate, and there he pulled off his muddy boots and went inside in his wet socks.

"Ward!" was the exclamation.

"I'm sorry Major but it's not possible to find out what happened in a detailed way, but it's bad I'm sure. Much of our artillery couldn't get into place, and some of those which did are having difficulty firing because of the mud, while their shells sink harmlessly into the mud. Our artillery didn't damage the pillboxes and I assume much of the wire was intact. Our machine guns won't work in the mud. The mud's very thick and it slowed the troops, which would be devastating under enemy machine gun fire. Some or maybe most tanks couldn't get through. Some men drowned, sir."

"They didn't stand a chance."

"No they didn't."

"I would like to send you away to clean up."

"It's alright; the battle's not over although it is lost."

Other Works by Mark Morey

The Red Sun will Come - June 2012

Souls in Darkness - August 2012

The Governess and the Stalker - July 2014

Maidens in the Night - September 2014

One Hundred Days

by

Mark Morey

Mark Morey

http://markmorey.blogspot.com.au

Copyright ©

I978-0-9944171-2-1

September 2015

ONE

It was an oppressive, humid day without a breath of wind, and with the sun beating down from a cloudless sky. Martin sat in the cockpit with his foot on the wheel of the small, white yacht while absent-mindedly brushing sweat from his forehead. In the cabin Louis and Sarah sheltered from the sun, while up forward Jara stared away into the distance. The diesel engine propelled the Esmeralda towards Normanby Island accompanied by a dull, rattling exhaust note and a light tang of fumes.

The faintest breeze momentarily rustled Martin's white shirt, and he looked over his shoulder at the Australian flag fluttering before sagging lifelessly. The breeze rustled again before fading, and then it returned even stronger. Martin left the cockpit and caught Jara's eye, and she helped him untie the mainsail from the boom. Martin went to the cleats and loosened the halyard before Jara helped him to haul the sail, and with a decent wind building the Esmeralda heeled over and turned to port. Working quickly they raised the jib and trimmed it tight. Martin returned to the cockpit and shut down the engine before re-setting their course, while to his right Jara trimmed the mainsail. She joined him in the cockpit just as Louis poked his head up the stairway.

"Come up and enjoy the freshness," Martin said.

"I shall," Louis replied, and moments later Sarah joined him on the deck. With the Esmeralda heeled over Sarah held a stay to steady herself. After the oppressive stillness, the wind against Martin's sweat-soaked shirt was fresh indeed. Poor Sarah, dressed as she was in a long, white dress with layers upon layers of underclothing beneath; even with the wind she would have been baking. Jara wearing a simple, knee-length red cotton skirt, a brief petticoat and nothing else, literally nothing else, was more practically attired for tropical weather.

"If this wind holds up we should reach Goba before sunset," Martin said.

Louis nodded and Martin knew the significance of an early evening arrival. There would be a feast for the doctor and his wife, the nurse, who would then be invited to stay in the village before they started their work the next morning.

"Are you coming ashore?" Louis asked.

"That's the custom," Martin said. "Kaikaim wantaim ples?" he asked Jara.

"Yes," she replied.

Louis nodded in acknowledgement while Martin checked the compass. With a good wind just a few points from their stern, the white yacht skimmed across the deep, blue ocean, parting a decent bow wave and cleaving a broad, white-tipped wake.

"I see it," Sarah said, pointing to the distance. Jara went to the stay while shading her eyes from the glare of the sun. The two women stood side-by-side; both about five foot two or three. Fair Sarah, blue-eyed with long, light brown hair braided and pinned beneath a floppy white hat, and Jara brown all over with short, dark, curly hair. After a while Martin spotted the green, misty mountains of Normanby Island. Right on course, and escorted to the village by men returning from late afternoon's fishing. A dozen or more canoes, each with two men, bringing home their catch which would form a feast in honour of the visitors from across the sea. The fishermen guided their canoes towards the beach while Martin got Jara to furl the foresail and mainsail, and under engine power he slowly drifted to what he thought would be a good anchorage about 30 yards from the shore. Martin put the engine into neutral and they drifted to a stop. He went forward to untie the anchor rope from the cleat, and then slowly played the rope out until the anchor caught on the sandy bottom, easily seen in the clear water. He tied the rope firmly before going to the engine and reversing slightly to get the anchor to hold. The rope was taught making a secure anchorage, and Martin led the way to the rope ladder at the stern and down into the dinghy. It only took a few minutes to row to shore and beach the dinghy safely.

The chief of the village, Tane, approached with his wife Masina. Louis and Sarah were first to be greeted, and once that formality was complete it was the turn of Martin and Jara, and briefly Martin pondered the unusualness of a young New Guinea woman being honoured by a village chief as an esteemed guest. But after four years of being an esteemed guest, Jara had adapted to her place in the scheme of things.

The village was close to the beach and consisted of two large, rectangular thatched huts: one for the men and one for the women, with a dozen or more smaller thatched huts of a similar style scattered about. One large, open hut served as a communal area, and there were a number of rough, timber benches adjacent to most of the buildings. Beyond was a cleared area for yams and other foods, and beyond that was dense, green jungle with spiky palm trees standing high at regular intervals. The village had a population of about fifty, split evenly between the sexes and covering all ages: from youngsters running about to the old, grey and wrinkled. Men of the village dressed simply with two brief bands attached to a belt at their waists: the front band hanging down to cover their genitals and the rear band covering most of their buttocks. Women wore full, knee-length skirts made from fibre; beneath were shorter fibre petticoats, and they were bare-breasted like Jara. Six young women gathered with six young men holding drums, and they broke into a dance of greeting which consisted of jumping and turning on the spot, and the women had lovely, sweet, harmonious voices for their song. The visitors were given cups of tangy, citrus drinks and were then led to the covered, communal area to await the feast. Martin knew older women of the village were baking in underground ovens. The feast was ready just before sundown, and while the older women brought the food on wooden plates, the young men and women performed a dance and song. The visitors were encouraged to eat heartily, and the fresh roasted fish, yams and breadfruit made for a lovely meal, especially with sweet voices in the background. Tane and Masina were served next, and then followed the rest of the village in order of seniority.

It had been a lovely feast, especially with the singing and dancing. Louis and Sarah stood and Tane stood to take Louis' arm. Martin went to them with Jara trailing. "Lukim yu behain," he said to all three as a farewell, and Jara said the same. The chief farewelled them with the same words while Louis clasped Martin and thanked him for the journey.

"I'll see you tomorrow my friend," Martin said.

"I'll see you tomorrow," Louis agreed.

Martin headed towards the dinghy and Jara helped him push it into the ocean. He rowed to the Esmeralda rocked gently at her anchorage, and hooked the dinghy in place before climbing the ladder. Jara followed him onto the deck where he took her in his arms.

"Mi laikim yu tru," Martin said, I love you, and he meant that too. The people of her country never travelled beyond their tribal lands, and yet she came with him to islands and settlements near and far, to tribes where she couldn't communicate except in Tok Pisin, where customs were strange and where she didn't belong. And he loved her for doing that and for everything.

"Mi laikim yu tru," Jara replied, but she didn't need to say that because Martin knew.

"We can wash in the sea," Martin said in Tok Pisin.

"Yes."

Martin unbuttoned his shirt and peeled it away while Jara removed her skirt before diving gracefully into the ocean in her petticoat. Martin disrobed to his underpants and followed Jara into the warm, tropical water; so refreshing. Jara came to Martin and wrapped her arms and legs around him while he held her soft buttocks. Her people didn't kiss except in the heat of passion, but that didn't matter. He held her and nibbled the side of her neck, and she bent her head to give him room. She squeezed him tighter before floating away and reaching for the rope ladder to climb on board. Martin momentarily admired his lover before joining her on the deck. Again she hugged him and again he nibbled the side of her neck the way she liked, before she broke off their embrace.

She led the way down the ladder into the compact galley with a bench, sink, stove and a box for coal on the right, and the table and benches opposite. Beyond an open partition was Martin's and Jara's sleeping area, with two benches running lengthwise topped by soft, thin mattresses, and storage spaces behind sliding doors beneath. A second partition had a sliding door to separate the second sleeping area which had a double bed, again with storage space beneath. Jara led Martin into that sleeping area which was fresh and cool with windows and the skylight open. She discarded her petticoat before lying on the bed, and Martin removed the last of his clothes before lying above her. He kissed her and sucked her lips and she bit him with delight before probing him with her tongue which he sucked greedily. He kissed her all over and she put her hands on his head before laughing and pulling away.

Jara sat up on the bed and Martin knelt in front of her, and then he pulled her to him while she wrapped her legs around his waist and held his shoulders. They made love mouth to mouth: slowly, unhurriedly, until her arousal took over and consumed all reason. She dug her nails into his skin; she bit his lips and dug him hard, scratching him even; closer, closer, all the way. She flopped onto her back and Martin took her hard, harder, harder still. Then in near exhaustion he collapsed on his lover and she cradled him gently. Naked they fell asleep in each other's arms.

* * *

Martin woke still intertwined with Jara, and as gently as he could he disentangled himself only she stirred. She woke smiling brightly as she always woke smiling brightly.

"Moning laikim," Martin said.

"Moning laikim," Jara said, before lightly touching his scarred lips with her finger while smiling even more brightly. "Fruit?" she asked in Tok Pisin.

"Yes please. Coffee?"

Jara shook her head. "No, no coffee," she said as Martin expected.

Martin shrugged his shoulders before going into the next cabin and taking a clean shirt and underwear from the storage compartment beneath his bed. He went up to the deck and pulled on his trousers, before tossing the red skirt at Jara who poked her head up the ladder. She disappeared for a moment before emerging to row the dinghy to Goba, and there she would be given enough food to start the day. In the meantime Martin placed the spirit burner on the coal stove and boiled water for his coffee. By the time he'd made a mug and taken it onto the deck, Jara returned carrying their breakfast of sago and bananas. They sat in the cockpit on a lovely, sunny morning with a faint breeze providing relief from the heat, and in the background was the endless roar of the sea rolling onto the beautiful, sandy beach. Later Martin went to Goba where he greeted Tane before seeking out Louis who already had a queue waiting for his clinic.

"Good morning," Martin said to the doctor and nurse, dressed officially in white and sitting on a rough, timber bench outside their borrowed hut.

"'Morning Martin," Louis replied while Sarah was busily engaged with a cooked breadfruit.

Martin sat beside Louis on the bench. "What are your plans?" he asked.

"I can do something for your lips if you want."

Martin touched where he was still sore, before deciding the villagers came first. "You can look at my lips later," he said.

"It'll take a couple of days here, and then we'll head south like last time."

Martin nodded in agreement and thought their journey would be about four weeks, like the previous year. It seemed surprising, no amazing, that he'd been to that village three times before. How time flew, but in his world time flew in the most delightful way possible. He had it all: the friendly peace and tranquillity of Melanesian village life, the advantages that came from being an Australian, and most importantly he had Jara.

"I'll arrange to take on fresh water and get the boat ready for the next leg," Martin said.

Martin headed off to talk with Tane while thinking that life was beautiful, and if was still sailing with his friends and with his lover in ten or even twenty year's time, then he would be the luckiest man alive.

* * *

After more than four weeks away it was good to return to Samarai, a busting, European-style settlement surrounded on three sides by impenetrable, tree-covered hills. The town had a grid of paved roads containing shops, bakeries, hotels, churches and many houses, while closer to the port were warehouses and trading companies. The buildings of Samarai were universally weatherboard, and almost universally painted white. With sails furled and under power from the engine, Martin guided the Esmeralda to the wharf space that he leased. At the last moment Jara jumped off with rope in hand to tie the boat forward, and then Martin tossed the aft mooring rope which she fastened to a bollard.

Martin tightened those ropes around their cleats to hold the Esmeralda tight.

Louis and Sarah bid farewell, and Martin knew they would be in a rush to get home to their real home. For Martin and Jara the Esmeralda was home, either sailing or tied up in Samarai. Although he was pleased to return to civilised life, especially to familiar food and drink, Martin sensed something was odd. A strange atmosphere and he didn't understand what or why. Then Louis returned and Martin guessed that he left something behind.

Louis climbed onto the Esmeralda and went straight to Martin. "We're at war," he blurted out.

"When, how?" Martin asked, confused.

"Archduke Ferdinand of Austria was assassinated in Serbia, and that dragged Austria, Hungary and Russia into conflict. Then Germany declared war on Russia before invading Belgium and France, so Britain declared war on Germany for invading Belgium, as did Australia."

Martin nodded slowly while he digested that news, and there had been talk of war with Germany for many, many years. But even after all that talk, actually being at war came as a shock. He wondered what he should do.

"I should go," Louis said, and he left the boat. Martin leaned against the rail of the Esmeralda and watched Louis head between the warehouses of the small settlement.

Samarai, the largest town in British New Guinea, under the administration of Australia; his homeland. His country was at war and many would enlist. He registered for military training when he turned 18 as was his obligation, while knowing there were no training facilities at Samarai. He shirked his duty once and didn't think he should shirk it again.

"Wanem olsen?" Jara asked.

Martin turned around to face his beautiful companion. "We're at war," he said in Tok Pisin.

"With who?"

"Australia's at war with Germany, but it's different to war here. Many will go to fight."

"Will you go?"

"If a tribe did the wrong thing and another tribe went to war, would it be right for a young man not to take part in the raid?"

Jara shook her head. "No it would not. Where is this war?"

"A long way away."

She took his hand and looked into his eyes. "Come downstairs and I will share pleasure with you before your journey."

Martin suddenly felt a burst of joy, but he wasn't going just yet. He earned his matriculation, and when he enlisted that could be an advantage. "I must write to my uncle first."

"You're not going now?"

"Not now."

"Then I will share much pleasure with you before your journey," Jara said seriously.

Martin squeezed her slim, brown hand lightly, and followed her to the ladder to their cabin.

TWO

The alarm rang with a dreadful noise and Alec reached out to turn it off. He lay with his hands behind his head while thinking about the past two weeks. So much had changed and his country needed him. He climbed out of bed and went to the bathroom, and then he dressed in his green militia uniform. After that it was time for breakfast in their modest kitchen; lovely and warm with the heat of the range. There wasn't much to the room: the range on one side, the sink and cupboard under the small window, a pantry to the left and a table with four chairs opposite. A modest room in a modest house in modest, suburban Melbourne.

Alec greeted his mother before sitting at his usual spot at the table. His mother cracked an egg on the frypan, and soon the room smelled of eggs and bacon. His father came in and Alec looked up. "Good morning Father," he said.

"Good morning Alec," he replied. "Your training...."

"You know I must train."

"I know, but remember that your career comes first. Until you get your apprenticeship I'm not signing enlistment papers."

"I know Father," Alec said. His country needed him but he had a five year apprenticeship in the way. His mother put a plate and a mug of tea on the table, and Alec grabbed his knife and fork for his bacon, eggs and toast.

"This war is by the rich and powerful against a threat to their wealth and status," Father said. "I left that behind when I came to Australia, and my new country has no business being involved in someone else's conflict, and the working classes have no business sacrificing themselves for rich capitalists. The working class of one nation are being set against the working classes of other nations, so the rich can get richer."

Alec had heard that many times but he didn't believe it. Germany invaded Belgium, a country not involved in any way, and that was simply wrong. "Yes Father I understand," he said.

"Do you?"

"I do," Alec said, even though he didn't.

"Are you going out tonight?" Mother asked to change the subject.

"I'm taking Dorothy to see a film."

"Make sure you're not home too late."

Alec sighed. "No Mother." Dorothy's parents wouldn't let her stay out late anyway. He finished breakfast and drank the last of his tea.

"Thank you for breakfast Mother," he said. "Goodbye Mother and Father."

Alec went out into a cool, cloudy day and walked to Mount Alexander Road with simple, detached weatherboard houses on his left and the oval on his right. He reached the main road with two shops on his left and the pub on his right, and in front of those shops he waited at the stop until a brown tram rattled into view. Bouncing and juddering and shaking. The tram stopped with squealing brakes and Alec climbed on board. The tram lurched underway and nearly threw Alec from his feet until he grabbed for a seat. The conductor staggered into view and Alec paid his fare to receive a flimsy paper ticket in return. The tram rattled along Mount Alexander Road busy with traffic, to the end of the line just before the depot building. There Alec climbed off with several other men in militia uniforms. They all climbed onto the waiting brown double deck bus, purchased tickets from the driver and were soon underway, heading west across the bleak outskirts of Melbourne, past windswept paddocks of weeds and thistles. The bus reached the Maribyrnong Training Centre where the real army trained. The army Alec should be joining, instead of militia training every second Saturday morning. Gunnery training with old artillery; using barrels so worn they never hit their targets. The war would be over before he could ever put his training to good use. He watched the men of the army drilling on the other side of the wire fence, until Sergeant Davies called them to attention. It was time to aim and fire.

* * *

Melbourne on Saturday night was busy and bustling, with streets and shops bursting with light. Alec doubted if there was a city in the world brighter than Melbourne on a Saturday night. He waited under the clocks at Flinders Street Station and looked all around, but there were too many women! Then she nudged him and took his hand. Alec kissed Dorothy's soft cheek and admired his darling, the love of his life, and he knew he was the luckiest man in Melbourne. No; the luckiest man in the world. Dorothy looked beautiful all in white: blouse, jacket, skirt, lace gloves and a lacy hat. He knew he looked the part for Saturday night, wearing his black suit, a white shirt, a black tie and a grey cap.

"Hello sweetheart," Alec said but maybe his voice was carried away by the noise of the crowd and the never-ending bells of trams trundling by.

"Hello sweetheart," Dorothy said. "How are you?"

"I'm fine; I had militia today."

"Do you have any plans for this evening?"

"There are new Charlie Chaplin films showing at the Ajax."

"That should be fun."

Alec took Dorothy's gloved hand, and together they went down the steps towards busy Swanston Street, and around the corner to the theatre. Alec bought two tickets and they went inside where it was very crowded. The films were funny as always, and were backed up by the Keystone Cops. The show lasted a couple of hours, and then they were heading outside with the crowd.

"Would you like something to drink?" Alec asked Dorothy.

"Yes please," she said.

Alec took Dorothy to a cafe and they went inside a long, narrow dining room in dull brown wallpaper, with a dark brown bench and a number of dark brown stools on one side, and opposite were several dark brown tables and seats built against the wall. It was crowded, smoky and smelled of chops and sausages, and fortunately there was a free table at the far end near half-louver doors to the kitchen. A young waitress came and they both ordered tea.

"I really liked 'Between Showers'," Dorothy said while looking hard at Alec. "Would you do that for me if the street was muddy?"

He took her hand. "You know I would."

"Would you fight over me?"

"Of course."

Their teas arrived and Alec added milk and sugar before sipping his drink. He was very thirsty. He admired Dorothy while she drank her tea: her flawless fair skin, her lovely, blue eyes and her soft blonde hair. But Dorothy was more than just pretty; more importantly she was thoughtful with a sharp mind. Dorothy was a special woman indeed.

"It's terrible this war with Germany," Dorothy said.

"It is," Alec agreed while unwilling to say more.

"Are you going to enlist?"

"I can't. I need Father to sign my papers and he won't."

"In a way I'm glad about that; I don't want you to be hurt. But how do you feel?"

"I think I should be enlisting but I don't have a choice," Alec said. "I'm sure the war will be over before I'm twenty-one."

"I'm sure it will be."

"I would enlist if I could."

"I know you would sweetheart."

Alec finished his tea and stifled a yawn. Dorothy finished her cup and looked up at him.

"We should go," Alec said. "I had an early start this morning and I'm quite worn-out." He stood and she stood and he took her hand, and together they navigated the crowds of Swanston Street while they walked to Flinders Street Station.

"Are you alright about not being able to enlist?" Dorothy asked.

"Germany's done the wrong thing and invaded Belgium, and of course Australia must intervene. I have militia experience and I know I could be of good use, but if I can't then I can't."

Dorothy squeezed his hand lightly. "I'm sure the war will be over before your twenty-one."

"I'm sure it will be," Alec said. Surely one country couldn't hold back the combined forces of Britain, France and the Empire for more than a few months. They reached the steps of Flinders Street Station and Alec kissed Dorothy's cheek. "Goodbye sweetheart and thank you for coming out with me."

"Goodbye sweetheart," she said. "Thank you for the evening and I really enjoyed being with you."

Alec stood at the base of the steps and watched until Dorothy disappeared out of sight. It was truly wonderful to have her as part of his life, and maybe one day they could marry. Alec was sure that would happen, and then he would be the luckiest man in the world. He turned away to catch his tram.

Even though Christmas was less than a month away, Melbourne's weather was cold, grey and miserable. Martin left the tram and crossed to the suburban shopping centre in Prahran, where one shop was adorned with several recruitment posters featuring soldiers, flags, the map of Australia, kangaroos and bugles. For a moment Martin thought he ought to give up on the idea and go back to his uncle's house, but it wasn't fair to expect others to carry the burden. He took a deep breath and went inside.

Four soldiers wearing khaki tunics, khaki breeches, khaki caps and brown boots sat at four tables, each with two simple chairs, and a further soldier was just inside the door. Opposite in the far corner was a timber screen, and along the walls were more patriotic posters.

"Can I help you?" the soldier at the door asked.

"I've come to enlist in the AIF," Martin said.

The solider nodded. "Go to that table and Sergeant Brooks will look after you."

Martin went to the nearest table and sat opposite Sergeant Brooks who picked up a form and a pen. Martin was asked his name: Martin Efrem Ward, his parish, town and county of birth, which said was Brisbane, Queensland, that he was a natural born British subject, twenty-two years and five months old, a sailor with matriculation and he was single. Martin gave his uncle as next of kin and his uncle's address, and he confirmed that he hadn't undertaken military or militia service, and that he was prepared to be vaccinated for small pox and enteric fever. The sergeant slid the enlistment form across the table and Martin signed and dated it the 30th of November, 1914.

Martin was taken behind the timber screen where a doctor in a white coat waited, along with a set of scales and a ruler attached to the wall. Martin was told to strip to his underwear, measured at five foot ten with the results called across the room, weighed at 11 stone six pounds, chest measured at 36 to 39 inches, complexion fresh, eyes grey, hair brown, vaccination on left arm and his denomination which Martin said was Church of England, even though he didn't believe anymore. Martin was poked, prodded; inspected everywhere, asked to cough while the doctor suddenly grabbed his balls which was a surprise, and eventually allowed to dress and return to the table where the doctor signed a certificate which proclaimed him fit for active service.

The last form was the oath to the King in the Australian Imperial Force effective from that date, and Martin signed that. Then he was then free to go. He went outside and waited for a tram, and about twenty minutes later he was at his temporary home in the leafy streets of South Yarra.

"How did your enlistment go?" Uncle Albert asked.

"I'm fit for service," Martin replied sarcastically while doubting that his uncle would recognise the sarcasm.

"What happens next?"

"I wait for a telegram."

The telegram duly arrived about two weeks later, ordering Trainee Second Lieutenant Martin Ward to report to Broadmeadows on the fourth of January for signals training and for officer training. He wondered if his uncle's contacts had anything to do with his rank, and with a job in signals, whatever that entailed.

Uncle Albert arrived home from his engineering consultancy a few hours later.

"You'll soon be rid of me," Martin said. "I commence training on the fourth for signals, and to be a second lieutenant."

"That's good for you," Uncle Albert said. "Signals are a specialist area which would suit an officer who hasn't militia experience."

Martin decided not to ask the obvious. At least he was going to be an officer and that would mean more money, which would help him when the time came to return to New Guinea and re-establish himself. With Australia already having defeated the German colony to the north of British New Guinea, opportunities for Australians had doubled in that part of the world.

"What are you thinking about?" Uncle Albert asked.

"What I will do after the war is over," Martin said.

"What will you do?"

"What I did before."

"Are you sure?" Uncle Albert asked, frowning.

"Yes."

THREE

Martin waited patiently in the line to receive his insignia, while to his left Harry was positively bubbling with energy or enthusiasm or maybe he just wanted to have a piss. Eventually Martin's turn came and he was handed the two strips of material adorned with single pips for a second lieutenant. Harry got his insignia, and having reached the end of the graduates, Major Bennet strode to a lectern where he gave a solemn speech about the important challenges facing each and every officer. After that they were dismissed and Martin wondered what came next. Until a young woman approached and kissed Harry's cheek.

"Congratulations darling," she said, and Martin knew the young lady was Edith, Harry's fiancee.

"Edith, this is Martin Ward," Harry said.

Martin took Edith's gloved hand and shook it lightly. "Good afternoon Edith," he said to the rather plain and slightly dumpy young lady who was the love of Harry's life. But she dressed well and had a nice smile, and Martin knew for a lifetime relationship it was much more important that she had a good heart. Harry was average more or less: average height at about five foot eight, average build, ruddy complexion and coarse, red hair.

"Good afternoon Martin," Edith said. "What's your future?"

"Training instructor like Harry, but signals rather than liaison."

"That's good for you."

With the terrible casualties at Gallipoli, being a training instructor was good news indeed.

"We've the rest of the day off," Harry said. "We ought to celebrate."

"We should," Edith agreed. "Martin, you should join us."

"I couldn't intrude," Martin said.

"Nonsense."

With that one word Martin had an invitation, and shortly after they were on a train heading south to St Kilda and the beach. Beaches brought back good memories.

"Martin, what did you do before the war?" Edith asked.

"I sailed a yacht out of New Guinea," Martin said.

"Oh really! That sounds so exciting!"

Martin leaned forward, closer. "New Guinea's the most beautiful and peaceful place in the world, and for four lovely years I had the most wonderful existence. But it was hard work and sometimes we had to sail quite long distances, and other times we hopped from settlement to settlement, so I was often close to shoals and rocks and looking for safe anchorages."

"I don't know anything about sailing but that does sound dangerous."

"With the right precautions it's not so dangerous, but you have to work at your sailing."

"Do you have a fiancee?"

"Edith!" Harry exclaimed.

Edith was forward, but getting engaged, getting married, buying a house with a mortgage and then having children was the Australian way. "One day I will return to New Guinea," Martin said. "And that's no place for an Australian woman."

"So the war followed by New Guinea?" Edith asked.

"Yes, and war means being posted in Melbourne."

"Training's just as important as fighting on the front line."

Martin knew that was true enough, but somehow he felt he ought to be doing more. He knew Harry felt the same way. The train rocked and rolled through the orderly suburbs of Melbourne, closing on the city centre which was busy and bustling as always. Once they reached Flinders Street Station on the banks of the muddy Yarra River, they used the subway to cross to the platform which would take them to their destination. They boarded another red train with Harry and Edith holding hands and Martin the outsider. Given he was based in Melbourne he would like to have a relationship, but with his future plans it would be unfair to court a woman and then abandon her. So for the meantime he was alone while surrounded by wives, fiancees and girlfriends. After a short ride they reached the sea, and Martin shouted them all ice cream cones before they took to the sand on a cool but sunny May day. Saturday the 29th of May, 1915. Germany, France, Belgium, Britain and Canada had fought themselves to a standstill in France and Belgium, while Australia, New Zealand, Britain and Turkey were slaughtering each other in Gallipoli. And in Melbourne, Second Lieutenant Martin Ward strolled along the beach beneath tall palm trees while eating an ice cream.

"I come from Brisbane," Martin said. "But when the weather's nice, Melbourne has its charms."

"It does," Harry agreed, and of course he would agree having never been further than the last tram stop on Sydney Road, or actually Broadmeadows Training Camp. "We came for a celebration," Harry said. "Thanks for the ice creams Martin, but we ought to have a proper celebration."

Martin wasn't fussed, and if his mate wanted a proper celebration before they returned for final muster, then so be it. They headed away from the beach towards The Esplanade which ran parallel to the seafront, and ahead was the grand, multi-storey Esplanade Hotel, overlooking the grey-green sea. Inside had dark blue walls and dark timber set against a dark, burgundy-coloured carpet. It smelt partly musty and partly of stale beer, and men leaned against the bar with pots of beer for company. Harry, Edith and Martin went to the lounge which was a bit less seedy, but only by degrees. Edith took a table and Martin sat opposite.

"My shout," Harry said. "What'd you want?"

"A shandy please," Edith said.

"A whisky please; no water no ice," Martin asked.

Harry went to the bar and Martin ducked outside to buy a special present for himself. He returned just as Harry brought a tray of drinks to the table, and Martin struck a match to play it over the end of his cigar.

"Mate, I didn't know you smoked!" Harry exclaimed.

"Just for special occasions, like graduating."

Martin breathed the sweet, woody smoke before resting his cigar on an ashtray and sipping his whisky. Now that was the life Martin thought, smiling to himself.

Over drinks they conversed about life in general, and after a second round of drinks, and steaks with mashed potatoes and boiled vegetables, it was time to leave. Together they caught a train to Flinders Street, where Edith and Harry chastely kissed farewell for they had different trains to catch to get to respective destinations. Some time later Harry and Martin were in their shared hut, lying on coarse sheets covering lumpy mattresses, and beneath thin, army blankets.

"Thanks for the invitation today," Martin said. "I had a nice time and Edith's a lovely woman. You're a lucky man."

"Thanks for coming with us mate; you're good company."

Martin enjoyed having company for the afternoon, and there was no doubt that Edith was a nice woman. Martin was sure that one day, they would have a happy, suburban, Australian existence.

FOUR

Martin sat on his bed and read the letter of bad news. He read it again and wished so much to change things, but forces out of his control had taken over. Instead he pulled out a pad and rested it on his knees while pondering what to write. Louis thought he was doing his duty by enlisting, but he was a married man and it wasn't fair to abandon Sarah just after she'd fallen pregnant. And the other news was inevitable after a year and a half apart.

'Dear Louis. Thank you for your letter and much has happened since I last wrote to you. I am pleased to hear that you will be parents and I am sure that you will be good parents. Of course you must leave New Guinea because that is no place for a mother to be, and I am sure that in Brisbane, Sarah will receive good care and attention. I was surprised to hear that you intend to enlist, and I understand that you wish to help the many casualties of this terrible war. I wish you the very best for your future in the AIF.

'My role has changed and I have been allocated to the newly-formed third division, and I sail out of Melbourne at the end of this month. We are bound for England and then we will be sent to the Western Front. Wish me luck for my future.

'I am pleased that Jara is married and she is pregnant too. My time with her was special to me, and she is a good person who will make a good parent for her child. I hope that she is happy with her new life.

'As a doctor in the AIF there is no doubt that you will be sent to the Western Front, so there is a chance that we may cross paths one day in the future. I hope we do. Until then take care.'

Martin signed and dated his letter the first of May, 1916 before placing it in an envelope. He held that envelope like it was the best part of his life coming to an end; just like that. He remembered their achievements and especially the good work they did for many villagers. He remembered the wonderful times they shared and in particular evenings on the yacht. The stories Jara told of her tribe's beliefs about creation, and when she ran out of those she made stories up which were even better. Ghosts and wars and lost children and always bitter-sweet. Endless games of pontoon once she mastered the arithmetic for cards, where she proved to be a good winner but a bad loser. After a year as a training instructor, being promoted to first lieutenant and being sent away to the theatre of war was good news. But his good news was dampened later the same day.

"What is it?" Harry asked.

Martin looked at his colleague, also promoted, also to be part of the third division and also to be sailing at the end of May. "I thought I was rid of you," Martin said. "But you hang around like a bad smell."

"You can't help bad luck. Do you know what we'll be doing?"

Martin put his envelope down and picked up his orders and re-read them. They both were allocated to divisional headquarters, rather than a company, battalion or brigade. That meant one thing. "There'll be a divisional commander and his staff, and we're part of his staff. So my role as Divisional Signals Officer must be to establish and maintain lines of communication between the commander and the brigades, battalions and companies of his division."

"Any my role must be to liaise between the divisional commander and other parties as regards supplies, transportation and armaments."

"That would be right."

"That could be interesting."

Martin crossed his arms while he thought about that, and that could be interesting indeed.

* * *

The tram shuddered to a stop on a wet, Friday evening. Alec climbed down at the safety zone; checked that the road was clear and crossed to the footpath. He went to that cafe in Swanston Street and Ruby was at a table, waiting. Alec went to her and she stood and kissed his cheek. He sat opposite and a middle-aged waitress came. They both ordered tea.

"How are you Alec?" Ruby asked.

"I'm good," Alec said. "How are you Ruby?"

"You're twenty-one tomorrow."

Alec nodded. "I am."

"You've been in the militia for many years...."

Alec knew what Ruby wanted to know. "I intend to enlist. Father made it clear that he's not interested in this war, so I have to wait until tomorrow to do my duty."

"Is it your duty?"

Alec leaned forward. "Right or wrong this country's at war, and my country needs me."

"You're my special brother and I'm worried what could happen."

"You're my special big sister and I'm worried what could happen."

"Then why go?"

Alec reached into his pocket and put the contents on the table. Ruby picked the bundle up and rolled them between her finger and thumb. "Seven white feathers," she eventually said. "These don't mean anything."

"Should I tune pianos while men my age go to fight?"

Ruby looked at the feathers again and sighed. "Be careful over there."

"You know me."

"I know you and you're better than just a piano tuner like your father. In another life with another family, you could have been special."

Alec nodded. "I know, but that was set."

"You have an advantage over many men there. Use that to your advantage."

"If I can I will."

Their teas arrived and Ruby sipped some before looking at Alec again. "Please write to me when you can."

Alec smiled. "A letter for my favourite big sister every week."

"I'll look forward to your letters coming every week." Ruby sipped her tea and sipped again. She then stood and went to Alec, and bent down and kissed his cheek. "You be careful Alec, and you know you'll be in my prayers every night."

Alec looked into her grey eyes. "That will mean a lot to me," he said, and he meant that with all his heart.

She left the cafe and Alec finished his tea before heading outside. Two doors along was a shop with posters, a shop he would visit the next day when he could. He paused and looked inside the darkened shop for a moment before crossing the road to catch a tram home. Later that evening was the same as any evening, until Alec told his parents that he was enlisting in the AIF tomorrow. He got sarcasm from his father about fighting rich men's wars, and worry from his mother which was only fair, and Alec went to his room early and read more of 'The Shadow-Line'. He went to bed early, waited for his father to leave for horse racing at Flemington before he got up and had breakfast. Alec then walked to Mount Alexander Road to catch a tram to the city. He went to that shop adorned with posters for the Australian Imperial Force, and just inside was a queue of four men with another two men being dealt with at two tables. Alec waited his turn.

Those waiting in the queue were dealt with one after the other, first at the tables then behind the two screens to the rear of the room. Alec moved to the head of the queue and the middle-aged sergeant told him to go to the table on the right. There a corporal waited with a pen in his hand and a pile of forms in front.

"Name?" the corporal asked flatly.

"Alexander Lillie Morey," Alec replied.

"How do I spell 'Morey'?"

Alec sighed. Always he was asked and it was a simple name. "M-O-R-E-Y," he said.

"And your middle name?"

42

"L-I-L-L-I-E."

The corporal wrote Alec's name. "Parish, town and county of birth?"

"Malvern, Victoria."

"Are you a natural born British subject?"

"Yes."

"Age?"

"Twenty-one today."

The corporal smirked before writing. "Trade or calling?"

"Piano tuner."

"Apprenticed at any time?"

"Allens here in Melbourne for five years."

"Married?"

"No."

"Next of kin?"

Alec gave the name of his father Alfred and his address.

He was asked about convictions, penal sentences or dismissal and Alec said 'no' to all.

"Have you served in the Militia?" the corporal asked.

"Yes, two and a half years field artillery, two years general duties."

"Still serving?"

"Yes."

"Sign and date here."

The corporal slid the form across and Alec signed and put the date; the sixth of May, 1916.

"Come with me," the corporal said, leading the way behind one of the screens where a doctor in a white coat waited.

Alec was asked to strip to his underpants and was measured. "Five foot six and a quarter," the doctor called out. Weighed. "Twelve stone nine," the doctor called out. Measured around his chest. "Thirty two and thirty four and a half inches. Fresh complexion, grey eyes, brown hair. What's your religion?"

"Church of England," Alec said.

"C of E."

The doctor examined Alec all over and even with a stethoscope. "Vaccination on left arm, scar on left knee, moles on the left shoulder blade and the small of the back. Fine, good," the doctor said. "You're fit for active service and you can dress now."

Alec dressed while the doctor went to the table, took a form from the corporal and signed it.

"Sit Alec," the corporal said.

Alec sat.

"This is the oath to the King in the Australian Imperial Force, effective from today the sixteenth of May," the corporal said. "After you sign this you're committed." Alec watched the corporal write Alec's name, the date, the place and state and the date again before sliding the form across. "Sign and date there."

Alec signed and dated the form.

"Good, you're free to go. You'll receive a telegram in a few weeks' time."

Alec left the recruitment centre and crossed to the safety zone on the other side of the street. There he waited for a tram to take him home. It didn't take long, twenty minutes, and Alec was home and sitting at the table in the kitchen.

"How did your enlistment go?" his mother asked.

"The army will send me a telegram in the next few weeks," Alec said.

Mother sat opposite. "Are you sure you want to do this? You know what your father thinks."

Alec leaned forward. "I know what Father thinks but Australia's at war, and if I don't enlist then who will? Is it fair to expect married men to leave their wives and children?"

"But you're engaged."

"And when I get back we will marry."

"I worry when I see the casualty lists in the newspaper."

Alec had seen the same lists. "I worry too," he said.

Mother took his hand and squeezed it. "Be careful," she said.

"You know I'll be careful."

"Of course you will."

"I'm well-trained and what the army needs." He looked into her eyes. "I have to do the right thing."

* * *

The telegram arrived a week later, instructing Trainee Driver Alexander Lillie Morey to report to the Field Artillery Brigade at Maribyrnong on Thursday the first of June at nine in the morning. Alec couldn't believe that! He knew everything about artillery and yet they allocated him to be a driver where he knew little about horses.

"What was that telegram?" his mother asked.

"I'm to report next Thursday for training as a driver," Alec said.

"Do you know what that is?"

"Drivers look after the horses and they ride the horses to bring the artillery into place, and they also bring shells to the guns."

"You don't know anything about horses."

Alec looked into her eyes. "I'm about to learn a lot more about horses." Alec thought he must see Dorothy one last time before his training. That Saturday night. For sure he would take Dorothy dancing on Saturday night. Alec heard the front door, and then he heard his mother tell his father about Alec being a driver and looking after horses. His father came to his room.

"I suppose if you know about artillery they put you in charge of horses, and if you know about horses they put you in charge of artillery," he said.

Alec nodded wryly.

"You're the one who wanted to enlist," his father said.

"You know the reason why," Alec said.

His father sighed. "I've never believed in this war as you know, but I understand the pressure brought on young men. You look out for yourself."

"Do I have your blessing?"

"You will be in my thoughts every day."

FIVE

The HMAT Berrmia steamed into Southampton harbour; a port on the scale almost beyond Martin's comprehension. Everywhere, all over, were docks and docks and more docks, with hundreds of troop ships and freighters tied up, and dozens of tugs scurrying about and belching dirty smoke. The Berrima slowed and a line was tossed to one of those tugs to haul them into a tight berth indeed, and it was a manoeuvre somewhat more complex than bringing the Esmeralda into Samarai and throwing a rope to Jara to slip over a bollard. Eventually the Berrima was secure and gangways run out, and the men were marched off the ship, officers first, and onto English soil or the harbour side actually. They were marched towards the city centre and reached the station where a train waited for the 500-odd arrivals. The new arrivals were shepherded into that train, officers first, and eventually the train pulled away.

Southampton was a busy, bustling city and very different to cities in Australia, which were slower-paced and more spread out. Martin gazed through the dirty window while they passed inner city buildings crowding narrow streets, buildings stained dark grey with soot and smoke, and further along they passed rows upon rows of terrace houses, also stained dark grey.

Even though Southampton was busy and populous, soon they left the outskirts and sped past lush, green pasture and crops. The land was undulating and looked very rich, which it needed to be to support a big population on a small island. Past villages with mixtures of the new and the ancient: houses, churches and more. Then more farmland before the next village, continuing north to their destination: Lark Hill. It wasn't far, about half an hour, and the train rolled past the little village of Amesbury and came to a stop at the railway station, which looked like any small railway station in Australia, except that it was in England of course. Built up high on a bank, the station consisted of a long platform with a multi-storey, brick station building with a canopy, and with more brick buildings to the rear, no doubt for freight. In the background was the neat and ordered village of Amesbury itself, where ancient cottages and an inn showed that time had largely stood still for a number of centuries. Martin and Harry followed the others out of the carriage and onto the platform where a number of officers and NCOs waited at the far end, with one of those NCOs holding a loud hailer. They were instructed to fall into line, officers at the head, and were led from the platform, through the outskirts of the village and along a road named The

Packway. They marched towards a large huddle of buildings on the rolling, green Salisbury Plains: Lark Hill Training Camp. The Packway had a chalky surface and footsteps raised dust, and soon Martin's eyes stung with the dust raised by more than 500 pairs of boots. The camp was quite massive and quite ugly, consisting of hundreds of large huts built from corrugated iron. They were led past a pitched-roof, church-like structure in corrugated iron to a large, flat, grassy area with the sign 'Parade Ground'. There they were lined up in order, more or less, to await the next challenge. A British lieutenant used a loud hailer to instruct the NCOs and the enlisted men to follow a sergeant to Camp Ten, while officers were requested to go to their billets in Camp One.

Returning along The Packway and to the right was Camp One, and barracks two was their home away from home, and basic it was with corrugated iron walls and exposed timber framing and roof rafters. Big, open and empty but for rows of beds which, upon inspection, were boards on legs topped by thin mattresses. Folded at the end of each bed was a sheet, a pillow in a pillowcase, and some grey blankets. It made the hut at Broadmeadows seem like the epitome of luxury. Martin sat on a hard bed and contemplated their circumstances. "The front will be worse than this," he eventually said as a consolation.

Harry nodded thoughtfully.

Suddenly the door burst open and a British senior officer strode inside. Startled, Martin didn't know what to do and then he did. He jumped to his feet and saluted, which was the right thing because the officer saluted back.

"At ease," the British officer said. "I am Lieutenant-Colonel Farmar and I will be the administration officer of third division."

"Lieutenant Martin Ward, Divisional Signals Officer."

"Lieutenant Harry Owen, Divisional Liaison Officer."

"Take a seat gentlemen."

They sat but not Lieutenant-Colonel Farmar. "I hope you had a good journey," he said.

"We did sir," Martin replied. "Or as good as months at sea can be."

"You were allowed off the boat?"

"A few times."

"That's good to hear." Farmar sat opposite. "We have learned much from the failures at Gallipoli and Pozières." he said. "The first is that Australian soldiers have to be trained to fight, to survive and to kill. We have fourteen weeks training allocated to third division. This will be broken down to four weeks company training, four weeks battalion training, three weeks brigade training and two weeks divisional training. Major-General Monash will be issuing orders regarding divisional behaviour over the next few days, and he will also be instructing companies, battalions and brigades about their training. Because you both are attached to divisional headquarters and because you both know your roles well being former trainers, the next few weeks may be quiet for you. I will arrange leave to Amesbury and you may wish to visit Stonehenge which I'm sure you will find interesting. As we get closer to divisional training, you both can rehearse your roles in mock battle situations, especially you Lieutenant Ward. There's nothing like taking out the telephone lines to make life interesting for the signals officer. In the meantime make yourselves at home, find the officer's mess, and in time you will be sharing this accommodation with other officers. That's all and enjoy your time here."

Farmar stood and left, and Martin watched him go. "Do you know anything about Monash?" Martin asked.

"A little," Harry said. "John Monash is ex-militia like me, and he saw action in Gallipoli where he was well thought of by his brigade."

"He must have been effective to go from militia to brigadier and now divisional commander."

"He must have been."

Martin pondered what came next, and finding the officer's mess was as good a place to start as any. "Well Harry, let's get something to eat. Later, we can play cards"

"You and your cards."

"Pontoon?"

"Alright mate."

* * *

Lieutenant-Colonel Farmar wasn't exaggerating when he said the first few weeks would be quiet for Martin and Harry. Day by day more enlisted men arrived at Lark Hill and were settled into corrugated iron huts before commencing their training, while officers were settled into Camp One and the huts there slowly filled. Martin observed from a discreet distance and it seemed that the infantry had learned little more than to stand up straight and march around parade grounds. They had to be trained in everything: to shoot, to bayonet dummies, to setup and operate machine guns, dig trenches, use trench mortars, fire artillery guns and more, much more. It was a sad indictment of the standard of training in Australia.

Beyond training Major-General Monash issued a number of orders, including full observance of the rules of saluting, which was something the infantry had been taught at least, and that the brims of their slouch hats were to be worn un-looped. That made sense and saluting was a good form of discipline. In time all would be expected to obey orders immediately and without question, and that obedience started with saluting NCOs and officers such as Martin, although in his role he wouldn't be ordering men to face death and destruction.

After a week of fine of weather where the fine, chalky dust got into everything, it rained and The Packway turned into a quagmire. It was terrible that the paths through such a major training facility became a sticky, gooey mess. Surely bitumen or gravel could have been laid. The lieutenants attached to battalions trained early until late, leaving Martin and Harry to play cards, watch films in the cinema when they were shown and generally waste time without appearing to waste time. They were given two day's leave to Amesbury and walked across the grassy plains to the strange structure called Stonehenge, which was an ancient place of worship or perhaps burial. That evening they stayed in the inn at Amesbury which was cheerful and friendly, and their rooms were seriously more comfortable than the cold, open hut at Lark Hill.

Lieutenant-Colonel Farmar gave Martin King's Leave for five days, and suggested that he should visit London. The next morning Martin purchased a second-class ticket at Amesbury and caught the morning train to Salisbury. At that sprawling station a London-bound train came through about a half-hour later, led by a smart, green locomotive hauling several brown carriages. Martin boarded an empty second-class compartment; the guard blew his whistle, the locomotive whistle squeaked in response, and they were on their way. The train rolled past a patchwork quilt of fields, some brown in fallow, raced past small villages and stopped at larger towns. The further they travelled the flatter the country became, until after about an hour when the train stopped at a large station at Basingstoke, the country was nearly featureless. They continued on and on until the train passed endless rows of terrace houses interspersed with shops and other buildings. They reached the suburbs of London: perhaps the largest city in the world and certainly the busiest and wealthiest. Slower and slower on bridges and viaducts until they came to a stop at the grand Waterloo Station, with many platforms sheltering beneath a massive, glass roof. Not so many travelled on that train, and Martin followed the small numbers of his fellow passengers along the platform, through a large concourse also nestling beneath a glass roof, and onto the street. There was a non-stop crush of pedestrians: men in expensive suits, ladies in lovely gowns, poorer classes in cheap or shabby clothes and some military men in uniform. Martin didn't know how to deal with the crowd but eventually pushed his way into the swarm. On the road, horses and carts, private cars, taxis and red omnibuses all fought for space. Nearby was the Wellington Hotel: no-frills, two-storey brick, and Martin went inside.

It was hushed and calm in the bar, dark with dark timber as hotel bars seemed to be the world over, and Martin went to the gentleman at the beer taps. He asked if they had rooms and they did, and a young lady showed Martin up a narrow, creaking staircase to a small room not dissimilar to the inn at Amesbury. Simple with an iron-framed bed, a timber wardrobe and a washbasin, and luxurious compared to the hut at Lark Hill. Martin unpacked his maps, left his kit on the bed, locked his room and went to the bar where he had a cheese sandwich and a cup of tea for lunch, before venturing into the crush.

On a beautiful sunny day, Martin followed his map by using one of the many bridges straddling the Thames: a broad, muddy river bustling with thousands of watercraft large and small. With the houses of Parliament to his back, Martin headed towards what he hoped was the Australian Soldiers' Club. There were many women and middle-aged and older men on the streets, not so many men his age, and clearly many men of fighting age were in France and Belgium. Unlike Australia, Britain had conscription for military service. Soldiers in khaki, identifiably Australian, showed Martin that he'd reached his destination. He had three full days in London and intended to make the most of his time by sightseeing as much as possible. He discovered they had free walking tours of the city sights, departing at ten each morning. He stayed inside where it was busy and noisy as all hell, and talked with some of the men on leave from the front, and while there he had a cup of tea even though he would have preferred something stronger.

After a couple of hours Martin took to the streets, and on the way back to his hotel he passed The Ship Tavern and went inside that pub. There, surrounded by glasses and beer taps, the middle-aged, moustached and yet bald barman in a striped white and blue shirt, surveyed all with his arms crossed. On a small blackboard on the bar was a menu, and Martin went to the barman and ordered a pork pie and a glass of red wine, and it could have been a pub in Australia except for the friendly acknowledgement 'right-o guv'nor'.

Martin took a seat at a small table near the window to wait for his dinner, which appeared some time later smelling deliciously and served with peas and mashed potato. It tasted as good as it smelled, and after that Martin returned to the bar to buy a whisky. At the table next to a window where it was night outside but bright with thousands of streetlights, Martin sipped his drink and watched the crowds. They all hurried past; everyone in London hurried as if their lives depended on it. A young, red-haired woman in a gold blouse, a red skirt and a white hat caught Martin's eye and he nodded to her in acknowledgment. She paused, nodded in reply, and Martin watched her come into the pub and head towards him. Like many women in England her dress was shorter than what was fashionable in Australia, and all the more attractive for that, and unlike many in London she didn't wear mourning black. On the ship they were warned of the dangers awaiting them, particularly in London, but Martin wasn't a naive young man from the suburbs of Melbourne or from a small, country town. He knew he could look after himself.

"Hello," she said, putting out her hand for Martin to shake it. "My name's Betty," she said in a coarse, London-like accent.

"Pleased to meet you Betty," Martin said, shaking her hand lightly. "I'm Martin."

"An officer?"

"Just a lieutenant."

She took her hand away and stood watching him. "Would you like a seat?" Martin asked.

Betty sat.

"Would you like a drink?" Martin asked.

"Yes please Martin," Betty said. "A gin."

Martin went to the bar and ordered a gin and another whisky, and took them to the table. He handed Betty her drink and she sipped it. "You're from Australia," she said.

"I am," Martin said. "I'm here on leave here for a few days."

"Then you must go to war."

"That's right."

"It'll be terrible like, to spend your last days of freedom alone."

Martin was surprised by her forwardness, but at the same time she didn't look like the women they were warned about. "I'm enjoying my time here," he said.

Betty finished her drink and Martin asked her if she wanted another, which she did. He bought one and she polished that off over small talk, and then a third.

"My handsome lieutenant from Australia...," she slurred, and Martin wondered if Betty had a drinking problem. It was getting late and Martin felt he should go, but he didn't want to abandon her as she was.

"It's getting late and we should go," Martin said.

"Naughty man...."

Martin drew a deep breath. "Can I help you to your home?"

She looked into his eyes. "You can help me anytime."

Martin got up and took her hand, and she slowly got to her feet and he led her out of the pub. Betty was able to give directions at least, even though she was somewhat unsteady on her feet. They went to Westminster Tube Station where Martin bought a return ticket to West Acton, before riding long escalators to a platform deep underground. Then followed a train ride where they had to change on the way, with the train emerging into open air after a time and just short of their destination. Betty lived in a street of duplex houses, with each pair of houses similar to each other pair of houses. Betty led Martin into a house where bedrooms and living rooms were converted into flats sharing a kitchen and bathroom, and she took him up the stairs. Her room was guarded by a brown door with the brass number five, and after several attempts to get her key into the lock, Martin took over and opened the door and turned on the light of a simple room with a bed, a chair, a wardrobe and a fireplace. During the course of their journey she had sobered up to some extent, but was still rather tipsy.

"Thank you my Australian lieutenant," Betty said in a somewhat slurred voice.

"I should go," Martin said.

"No! Don't!"

Martin was surprised. "Are you alright?" he asked.

She sat on the bed looking totally miserable. "No I'm not alright. I met a man an' he told me he would marry me an' take me to Australia, but...."

Martin was shocked. "I'm not like that," he said.

"That's why I drank with you. You're nice."

"Thank you."

"It's cold in here, don't you think?"

Martin thought that it was rather cold for a home, but the fireplace was set with kindling and newspaper, with a bucket of coal to one side of the hearth. "I will light the fire for you and then I must go."

Martin knelt on the polished floorboards and struck a match, and soon the kindling was blazing. He put on a couple of lumps of coal and wiped his hands on a rag hanging over the side of the bucket. He stood and turned around to face Betty. "I really should go," he said.

"Where're you staying?"

"Near Waterloo Station."

"It's late to be travelling that far.

Martin checked his watch and got the most awful shock; it was past ten. "I must go."

"You won't get back in time."

"What else can I do?"

"You can stay here."

Martin pondered the double bed and knew he couldn't; especially with a woman who'd drunk too much and who'd been taken advantage of before.

"We can share but nothing'll happen," Betty said.

"Are you sure?" Martin asked.

"You have no choice. I'll wear my nightgown and you can sleep in your underwear."

Martin nodded slowly while thinking that would work.

"I must dress so you turn around," Betty said.

Martin did as he was told, and contemplated the fire before putting more coal on the flames and wiping his hands. He heard the bed springs creak and turned around to see Betty on the far side, near the wall.

"Your turn," she said.

Martin sat on the bed and removed his boots, then his tunic, breeches and shirt, and draped them over the chair. Then he removed his socks, which he poked into his boots. Martin turned off the light and slipped into the cold bed.

"Night 'n all Martin," Betty said.

"You too," Martin replied, but he doubted if he would sleep. He lay in the near-dark in a strange bed and wished that sleep would come, because it had been a very long day.

* * *

Martin woke to the wail of a siren with the note rising and falling, and he wondered what that could be. Explosions followed and artillery fire too. Betty suddenly sat up.

"Zeppelins," she said. "Let's see." She got up, went to the window and pulled the curtains open. Martin stood alongside her and watched searchlights probing the clear, night sky. Then, momentarily, a massive, silver shape was caught in the light before slipping out of view, only to reappear moments later. Martin watched artillery and machine guns fire at the silver airship, he saw fine strips of light from tracer bullets before the Zeppelin disappeared from sight once more. More explosions and then more artillery fire, and it was like cat and mouse games between airships and artillery crews defending London. It went on and on; searchlights finding their targets and the gun crews responding before losing sight once more.

"Look," Betty said. "There's a plane."

Sure enough there were two aircraft; absolutely dwarfed by a Zeppelin targeted by a searchlight. And a glow of red in the distance with a part of London burning. Martin watched, transfixed, as searchlights wandered the sky searching for enemy craft. More explosions with the house momentarily vibrating from bombs landing maybe a few miles away. Shortly after another glow of red appeared not so far away; very close to Acton in fact. Searchlights picked out a Zeppelin and the artillery opened up, but as always the airship continued to drift across the sky unharmed. And then Martin saw a tiny aircraft beneath the huge, silver craft; Samson versus Goliath.

"Look over there," Martin said, holding Betty's arm and pointing.

"I see it," she said. "The pilot's so brave."

Martin thought the pilot was a brave man indeed. A Zeppelin must have many machine guns and all were aimed at that little aircraft, while searchlights lit the night sky and artillery fire continued unabated. The aircraft flew lengthwise underneath and then looped around and headed towards the tail of the Zeppelin. And then, slowly, the rear of the Zeppelin glowed red and moments later the airship was ablaze from end to end. No more searchlights and no more artillery either, and still blazing the airship slowly sank out of sight accompanied by flares glowing in the night sky.

Martin leaned against the window sill with his heart beating fast. "They got one at least," he said.

Betty grabbed his arm. "They did," she said almost breathlessly.

"Does this happen very often?"

"About once a month."

"It's wrong to bomb innocent civilians."

"It was wrong to invade France an' Belgium." She squeezed his arm tight. "You're fighting for a good cause."

"I haven't fought yet," Martin said.

"But you'll fight an' you'll win."

"Right must prevail," Martin said; honestly believing that to be true.

Betty took his hand. "Let's go to bed."

Martin allowed Betty to climb into bed and he followed her to lie beside. Martin checked his watch and the glowing hands and numbers showed it was almost three in the morning. He rolled onto his side and closed his eyes; willing sleep to come. But sleep didn't come; so in the semi-darkness with light from the fire and from the open curtains, he waited for morning. The sooner morning came the better, and then he could get out of the strange situation he'd found himself in.

He heard a noise outside their room, and even worse he heard someone at the door. The lock clicked and a man burst into the room. Martin sat up to face the stranger: tall, broad, muscular; aged about thirty in a white shirt, black waistcoat, black trousers and a grey cap.

"What's goin' on 'ere," the stranger boomed.

"Who are you?" Martin asked.

"What're you doin' with me missus."

"She's your wife?" Martin asked; confused.

The stranger stood next to the bed: scowling and looking dangerous.

"Look mate; nothing's happened," Martin said. "She got drunk, I helped her home and then it was too late for me to...."

"Wasn't too late to fuck her," the stranger interrupted.

"I didn't."

"Billy, he did," Betty said.

"She's lying," Martin said, while wondering why Betty said that.

Martin made to climb out of bed but the stranger, Billy, pushed against Martin's chest so hard that Martin couldn't move. He was a strong bastard. Billy pulled a razor out of his pocket, unfolded it and held the blade against the side of Martin's neck with cold, sharp steel that could cut his throat in a second. Martin's heart raced so fast that it seemed like it would explode, and he knew he was no match for Billy, with or without that razor. Billy was too strong and seemed like a fighter, which Martin wasn't.

"You're in me bed with me missus," Billy said clearly and calmly.

Foggy thoughts parted and Martin guessed what was up. "What do you want?" he asked.

"Everythin' you've got."

"That's not much."

Billy grabbed Martin's clothes and turned them over before finding Martin's wallet, and rifling the pockets before throwing it across the room. "Where's your money?" he snarled.

"I've only got a few shillings."

"How can you come to London with just a few shillin's?"

"You've been through my clothes and that's all I've got." Martin eased out of bed, went to his tunic and opened a pocket. He took out two coins and gave them Billy. "That's all there is."

"Fuck Betty!"

"How was I to know?" she said. "At least I got a few drinks out of him."

"Shut-up!" Billy glared at Martin. "Get out of 'ere," he growled.

Martin dressed as calmly as he could, and when he dressed he crossed his arms and looked at Betty. "This could go badly for you one day," he said. And then he eased behind the Billy still holding the razor, and went into the hallway and closed the door behind.

He waited for a moment and heard voices from the room. "I can't do this no more," Betty said. "I need a few drinks like to get courage up, an' I ended up drunk."

"You'll do as I say," Billy snarled at her.

"You know what happens with some of 'em."

"So what if they fuck you?"

"I'm not a whore Billy."

"You're me wife an' you'll do as I say."

"You got, what, a shilling?"

"Last time we got ten pounds. I'm tired and I want to sleep."

"Where were you?"

"Never you mind where I was."

"You got other women doing this."

"An' they're better at it than you."

"I'm you're wife."

"An' that's why you'll do as I say."

Martin had heard enough. He went down the staircase to the street where the early, dawn light glowed red in the distance. Poor Betty. She'd married a man who probably seemed better than he was, and was trapped in a loveless marriage where he misused her in the worst possible way. But like all married women she couldn't divorce him unless she proved physical abuse, no easy thing, so Billy was right. She would do as he told her.

Martin retraced the route to West Acton station, showed the return portion of his ticket to the porter at the gate, and then waited on a bench on the platform. He felt sorry for Betty and he wished he could do something for her, but even if he did there were thousands or maybe hundreds of thousands of married women in dire straits in that city alone. At least Martin got out of his situation lightly. Taking notice of what they were told on the ship and from the posters at the camp, he drew only enough pay for a few days leave, and he left most of that money concealed in his kit in his hotel room. In the end it cost him three glasses of gin, a return ticket to West Acton and one shilling and sixpence. Martin stretched and yawned just as a tube train approached, and he looked forward to getting to the Wellington Hotel. There he would take a bath, change his shirt and underwear, and after breakfast he would be ready for his walking tour of the sights of London. The train squealed to a stop and Martin went into a nearly empty carriage, not surprisingly empty given it was quite early. The train whined away from the station and Martin thought about what he could do for the rest of his leave. His father's family, his family, came from Maidstone in Kent, only a short train ride from London, and Martin decided to visit that town and maybe find some distant relatives. Then he would catch up on any sights not covered by the walking tour, especially museums and art galleries, and that would make for a worthwhile excursion to the largest, busiest and wealthiest city in the world.

* * *

Martin was in no hurry to return to Lark Hill, and he caught an afternoon train to arrive at Amesbury after dark. After a typically dreadful meal in the Officer's Mess, he was back to their cold, inhospitable hut in Camp One. Martin removed his boots and tunic and lay on his bed, because there was little else to do.

"How was London mate?" Harry asked.

Martin wondered how much to say, and he was embarrassed recount his adventure with Betty and Billy. "The sights are good," Martin said at length. "It's worth a visit for sure."

"Anything else?"

"There was a Zeppelin raid the first night I was there, and I saw one get shot down. It burned in the sky."

"They're full of hydrogen and that's very combustible."

Martin didn't know that. He decided that if Harry was given leave and went to London, he would forewarn him, but otherwise he didn't need to recount his rescue of the drunken Betty and what followed.

"The King's coming to visit," Harry said.

Martin groaned. "Not another parade."

"And rehearsals."

"When's the visit?"

"The twenty-seventh."

Martin yawned. "I'm quite tired and I might turn-in."

"Travel does that."

"I did a lot in five days."

Two day's later they had their first rehearsal for the King's visit, and a second rehearsal the following week. On a cloudy Wednesday the 27th of September, the entire division of 27,000 men was assembled for inspection by the king on horseback, accompanied by Major-General Monash and his senior staff. The king's inspection took two, long hours because of the immense size of the force, and once again the Australian parade ground training came to some use. Once again Martin's parade ground training came to some use. After the two rehearsals; the day went smoothly indeed. Unfortunately, shortly after the inspection was finished, the rain bucketed down, and 27,000 men were thoroughly soaked by the time they got to respective huts. They were not happy, even if it had been the king. Martin thought the time spent preparing for the inspection would have been better spent getting the division to the front a few days sooner.

Just over two weeks later the division voted in what was called a referendum on conscription but was really a plebiscite, and Martin voted against the idea. Those who wanted to fight in lands far away from Australia were free to enlist, and that was the end of it as far as he was concerned. A few weeks after that was the great mine explosion exercise, by which time the plebiscite had been defeated in Australia. Then divisional exercises were held, and Martin was busy at last dealing with communications the Major-General John Monash way, which like many things wasn't what was taught in Australia. But they worked so that was one good thing.

Finally after some drawn-out and lengthy marches it was time to depart, and like everything, departure from Lark Hill took planning and organising on a truly, massive scale. Being divisional headquarters staff, Martin and Harry were amongst the last to leave after regular train departures from Amesbury to Southampton over six days. From there they caught ferries to Le Havre bound for Armentières in northern France, railhead Steenwerck, close to the border with Belgium and just over 10 miles to the south of Ypres. They were to be a part of the Second Army under the command of General Herbert Plumer.

SIX

Martin closed on the front lines amidst a bustle of activity. Infantry strolled towards Bailleul for their relief, many of the men smoking, and Infantry returned to the lines after relief, many of the men smoking. Engineers worked on a timber pathway, duckboards, across the muddy, mushy ground. Muddy wasn't the right description and it was as much brown water as it was mud. To the right was a destroyed cart and two dead horses, abandoned where they fell, and beyond that was an overturned truck. In the near distance to the left were the remnants of a wood, with bare and mostly dead trees pointing at the sky. Further on to the right was the shattered town of Armentières with narrow streets lined by mostly brick buildings, straddling a river which ran through the centre of the large town. Still populated by a few hardy civilians from what Martin could see, even though they were less than a mile from the front line. Every now and then a German shell whistled in and there was much scurrying about until it exploded, making yet another crater in the pock-marked landscape. A driver assisted by another driver on foot, drove his horses along another formed road coming in from the right. His cart was loaded with shells, and the horses struggled with the weight of their load and with the mud, even though it was a proper road lined by dead trees. And then there was that ominous dull whistle and the driver on foot threw himself to the ground. Martin ducked instinctively and moments later there was a massive explosion which threw dirt high in the air, and the dirt and mud sprayed over Martin some 30 yards away. Martin watched in near disbelief as the driver climbed from his cart and ran to his mate on the ground, writhing in agony and clutching his right arm. Martin struggled across the muddy, marshy ground along with several infantrymen. They reached the injured man with his arm all but cut in half.

"Get the stretcher bearers!" a voice ordered, and Martin felt useless because he didn't know how to do that. A young soldier went away while the horses shrieked in pain. They were badly injured indeed.

"Shoot the bloody horses!"

Martin reached for his pistol just as several shots crackled out and the shrieking stopped. Then two men adorned with white bands with red crosses came to the scene carrying a stretcher. The injured soldier was lifted onto that stretcher with his almost severed arm placed carefully, and he was carried away. The infantrymen returned from whence they came leaving the driver alone with a cart and two, dead horses; the driver literally scratching his head. He plodded back along the road to the west, towards the railhead at Steenwerck where the horses were stabled, presumably to get more beasts to carry his burden. Martin's heart beat fast and he wished he could have done something, but the men of the front lines knew what they needed to do and they did it well. He had his role and it wasn't ferrying shells or carrying the wounded, so he took a deep breath and picked his way across the brown ooze towards the duckboards, sinking almost to his knees with each step. Once on the timber pathway the going was much easier, and closer to the lines and sheltering beneath camouflage nets were the eighteen pounders of third division. They were mostly silent although two crews worked at answering the German shells being sent across at random intervals. Martin carefully stepped off the timber and watched them at work: one gunner at the right aiming, one gunner on the left with the trigger, three gunners loading shells from a stockpile behind the gun and one dealing with the used casings. The shells were passed hand to hand and then fed into the gun before firing with the most incredible explosion and recoil, then the breech was opened and the still steaming casing fell out and was tossed aside before the process was repeated.

Martin continued forwards where there was terrible smell getting stronger, until he reached the reserve trenches, so-called. The ground was naturally flat and

75

marshy and had been drained by rivers and man-made canals, until shelling by both sides destroyed those rivers and canals, turning the battlefield into marsh again. There was no hope of digging a trench in oozing mud, so the trenches were mostly of timber framing supporting wire netting and sandbags filled with clay. Trench flooring was timber duckboards although the ever-present mud and water oozed everywhere, making the trench a sodden, murky mess. Men spent several days in the front line trenches conducting patrols, fending off any German raids and conducting raids of their own, before resting in the support and relief trenches at the rear for several more days, assuming they could rest with the noise of the near-continual artillery and trench mortar fire from both sides. After that the men would get several days billeted away from the front lines before returning to deal with mud, snipers, raids, trench mortars, random artillery shells and sickness. Martin was there for a purpose and he headed to the left to find the signals dugout of thirty-seven battalion.

He squeezed past lounging soldiers while following the zigzagging above-ground trench. Zigzagged so that if a shell landed it one section the blast wouldn't go beyond that section, and if the enemy were to breach their defences they couldn't fire machine guns from end to end. Squeezing past lounging soldiers not the least bit concerned about the many, big, black rats running by.

Eventually Martin reached the above-ground dugout: rough timber walls, a corrugated iron roof and well protected by sandbags. Martin brushed the gas curtain aside and went into the dark and damp space lit by a candle, with a knocked-together bunk bed on one side, and a rough shelf with some shaving gear and a small mirror on the other side. Pride of place was the trench phone on a second shelf. He saluted a captain before seeing Alfred on a rough chair beside a handmade table and drinking a mug of tea. Alf was one of his trainees from Broadmeadows.

"Hello Alf," Martin said.

"G'day mate," was the response. "What can I do you for? You want a brew?"

"No thanks mate. I'm after some feedback on the raids you've conducted over the past while."

"Feedback on communications?"

Martin nodded. "Yes," he said, taking a rough, handmade chair opposite.

"It's too hard," Alf said shaking his head slowly. "When the men go over they're exposed and they can't defend themselves."

"How so?"

"You can run or you can stop and shoot, but you can't run and shoot."

That made sense and that made crossing no man's land really hazardous, or just random chance that you would make it to the other side. "How are communications when they go over?"

Alf frowned. "We use periscopes which don't give a good view, but mostly we rely on runners. The thing is the mud's hard to cross at the best of times, so it's hard for runners while struggling through mud with Huns shooting at 'em."

"Is it possible all runners could be killed?"

"Yes."

Just then two big, black rats ran through the dugout, and Alf didn't show the least bit of concern while he sipped his tea. "Where do these rats come from?" Martin asked.

"They feed on the corpses in no man's land. Can't you smell 'em?"

Martin suddenly felt sick. He took a deep breath and another and stared at the table for focus. "For a raid maybe to the minute communication isn't so vital, but for a battle with reserve forces, keeping HQ informed could be the difference between success and failure."

"I know mate, I know."

"But that's my job and not yours, and thanks for the information."

"Any time mate. Just drop by and pay a visit." Alf studied the table. "You were the best," he said quietly.

"I'm glad out of all that training I gave; I have a good mate on the front lines. See you later Alf."

"See ya mate.

Martin retraced his steps out of the lines fortunately without any more drivers being shelled, and thought about options for their problem with runners. Eventually Martin reached the iron fence surrounding Chateau Steenwerck, which was the divisional headquarters shared with Monsieur and Madame Plouvier. Although some miles from the front, the sound of artillery carried to the chateau clearly and distinctly; a never-ending reminder of death and destruction so close. Martin passed through the open, iron gates into the unkempt garden and went to a tree on his left where a large twig or small branch had fallen on the ground. He used that twig to scrape the mud from the soles of his boots before proceeding along the short path to the large but simple chateau: a square, two-storey building in brick, and with a series of attic windows beneath a low-pitched slate roof. He climbed the three steps, opened the door and went inside. Immediately to the right was the sitting room and he went in there to see the General Staff Officer, Major Wylly, comfortable in an armchair while reading some papers. Martin saluted smartly and Major Wylly stood to return the honour before Martin stood at ease.

"Ah Lieutenant Ward," Major Wylly said, putting his file to one side. "What do you think of our lines?"

Before he left Australia, Martin had researched the Somme and the Flanders battlefields, but that research hadn't prepared him for the reality of what he saw. "If we wished to pick the absolute worst place to fight a war, this would be it," Martin said.

"That's true, but fate has dealt us this hand."

"It's as bad for the enemy as it is for us, so we're equally compromised."

Major Wylly nodded slowly. "You're quite right with that observation, although the enemy is more likely to advance in the south towards Amiens and Paris rather than expend effort here."

"We must keep them pinned down here or else we open a way to Paris from the north, although we could never win an offensive campaign in this mud."

"That's true as well. Take a seat and tell me what you think."

Major Wylly took his seat and Martin sat in the other, burgundy-coloured leather armchair, which momentarily felt surreal. "Our best form of communication remains telephone lines to brigades, battalions and companies," Martin said. "We can easily relay orders and they're easily understood compared to Morse. I assume in such a well-established battlefield, our telephone cables are well underground to minimise damage from shells. However, if we were to undertake attack on this muddy, marshy ground, to rely on runners to relay messages to battalion headquarters to be telephoned onwards is risky. Just walking on this ground is difficult, let alone expecting there to be unbroken lines of communication. I recommend that we augment our usual system of runners and telephone with aerial observation. Not just artillery spotting but Morse messages transmitted from the battlefront using signal lamps, and re-transmitted by observers on planes or balloons using wireless sets. We could also have wireless transmissions of battle progress as seen by observers as they fly overhead. That way headquarters can keep track of the battle and take action where necessary."

"Such as sending in reserve troops to assist where there's trouble?"

"That's right. Because wireless is in short supply and it takes some expertise to operate it, the aircraft or balloon observers should send wireless messages to our battle headquarters, and from there we can relay relevant orders by telephone to brigades and battalions. This way we aren't relying on runners, which I believe are our weakest link."

"I will keep this in mind, but I don't expect there to be any battles until spring at the earliest."

Martin knew winter weather and the condition of the battlefield worked against major offensives in the short term, but he doubted that third division would merely wait out the next few months. After all that training and especially with Major-General Monash so proud of his division, action of some sort was inevitable.

"Thank you for your report Lieutenant," Major Wylly said. "Now I'm sure you would like to clean up. After setting up the switchboard and now this, you ought to take a break for this evening. Go to Bailleul if you wish, and take Lieutenant Owen with you."

Martin was splashed with mud from head to toe and he certainly needed to clean up. "Thank you sir and I shall," he said.

Martin stood, saluted and went outside to one of the simple, rectangular timber huts in the grounds of the chateau. His basic lodgings; inevitably shared with Harry. He went inside their room which contained two camp beds and two foot lockers.

"You look terrible!" Harry exclaimed.

"Thanks mate," Martin said. "You should go for a reconnoitre."

"It's obviously muddy, like everywhere around here's muddy."

"You can get blown up too."

"And you thought headquarters was safe."

"It's safer but not safe." Martin lowered his voice. "I saw a driver get injured by a shell. It was terrible."

"That could have been you."

"Thirty yards and it could have been. Harry, do you want to go to Bailleul? Major Wylly's given us the evening off."

"Of course."

"I'll clean up as best I can, and then we can head off for a night on the town."

* * *

Bailleul was a decent sized, well-established town which benefitted from being close to the front, but not so close as to be shelled and destroyed. But close enough for the sound of artillery fire to be heard, and Martin hoped that one day he would get used to that sound. Close enough for the flares fired from both sides to be clearly visible, and those sudden bursts of bright, white light were a particularly eerie sight in the night sky. With a tragic war so close the streets of Bailleul bustled with hundreds of British, Canadian,

Australian and New Zealand officers, NCOs and enlisted men; some quiet, some happy, some boisterous and a small number quite drunk. Bailleul radiated outwards from a large, cobbled square which contained a large church on first glance, but given the steeple-like structure contained four clock faces; it was actually the town hall. Adjacent to the town hall were many shops with not so many goods for sale given war shortages, and each shop had a distinctly different architectural appearance to each other shop, which was rather unusual. Overall the style was hard and angular which was quite different to other towns in France, and many of the buildings were in red brick, again quite different to other towns in France. There were many cafes, bars and restaurants, and further away from the square were premises with red lights and premises with blue lights sharing narrow streets with multi-storey houses and apartment buildings. At some red light premises, NCOs and enlisted men queued outside waiting their turns. There was pushing and shoving when some Australians, identifiable their untidy clothing, went to the front of a queue and were able to get in. Australian infantrymen, gunners and drivers earned five shillings a day while their British counterparts had to survive on a miserable sixpence.

"There's a brothel," Harry said, stating the obvious.

"For enlisted men," Martin clarified. "Officers get a blue light. Are you interested?" Martin asked mischievously.

"Aaah..... Who knows how long it will be?" Harry said quietly.

"I was joking."

"Oh."

"Let's get some decent food and something to drink, and then catch up on a show or film. I believe there's an officer's club somewhere."

They returned to the square, and eventually found a cafe that wasn't too crowded, and went inside to a room in burgundy-coloured wallpaper with about a dozen mahogany tables and chairs squashed close together, and a mahogany bar along the side wall which had many glasses hanging upside down above. A young waitress showed them to a table and left two menus, and Martin browsed what was on offer.

"I'll have a steak and chips," Harry said.

"You might have trouble with that one mate," Martin suggested, because the menu was in French and it was all local cuisine. "I can order you something similar."

Harry frowned at the menu. "Alright then," he mumbled.

"Beer?"

"Yes please."

The waitress returned. "Bonsoir Mademoiselle," Martin said. "Je voudrais un verre de Riesling et quiche Lorraine, et d'une la bière et potée Lorraine pour mon ami."

"Certainement Monsieur," she said before leaving.

She returned with their drinks a few minutes later. Harry looked pleased with his beer, and even more pleased with his hotpot, or stew in Harry-speak. It looked hearty and filling and tasty, while the quiche with salad was light and delicate and far removed from army rations.

"You know the blue lights...?" Harry asked between mouthfuls.

"I know of them," Martin said, having discovered that as part of his research.

Harry put his knife and fork down and looked Martin in the eyes. "We're here and they're there," he said quietly.

Martin nodded, and it had been a long, long time. But he doubted, no knew, that after his time with Jara, anything in such an establishment would be a disappointment. But one thing he missed more than anything was touch, and his only touch was the odd, firm handshake. He really missed touch, and Harry was right earlier that evening about how long it would be. "I know what you mean mate," Martin said quietly. "But for tonight the Canadians have set up a theatre which alternates live shows and films, and after this good food, that theatre would make for a decent evening, don't you think?"

"It would." Harry tucked into his stew again. "What's this called again?"

"Potée Lorraine. Quite literally local produce thrown into a pot and stewed for a few hours."

"I got to hand it to the Frenchies."

* * *

That night Martin lay in his bed listening to the never-ending crump, crump, crump of artillery fire. He rolled onto his side and closed his eyes, and he remembered the driver writhing in agony with his arm hanging uselessly. Martin rolled onto his other side and hoped that sleep would come.

SEVEN

Alec didn't plan on arriving in England on a stretcher, but he didn't plan on an outbreak of dysentery on HMAT Borda either. There they were, eleven quite sick, lined up on stretchers and waiting to be carried down the gangway after the rest of the men, some 500 or more, disembarked by conventional means.

A doctor in a white coat accompanied by four men in uniforms strode up the gangway and came to where they waited.

"Hmm," the doctor said. "Dysentery. No wonder with so many men cramped together. It's a wonder we don't get more." The doctor turned to the four men in uniforms. "Take them to Devonport Hospital."

The doctor left.

"Tryin' to get out of it before you've even started?" one of the men in uniform said cheerfully while smiling brightly. "Don't worry. After a week or so you'll all be right as rain and ready to be trained for Flanders."

"If you can get us off this ship...," Terry grumbled.

"I can only do two at a time but the hospital's not far. We'll start with you two."

One of those two was Alec and the other was Jack, and soon Alec and Jack were carried down the gangway and into the back of an ambulance parked at the Plymouth dockside. The port of Plymouth was big, bustling and busy, and it made the port of Melbourne, where they boarded the Borda some two and half months previously, seem insignificant by comparison. The ambulance rattled away and about ten minutes later the rear doors opened to reveal a large, old, granite building surrounded by trees and lawns, and beyond the gardens was a big granite wall hiding all from general view. Stretcher bearers in white coats carried Jack and Alec up grand, timber stairs with their noisy boots echoing in the big entry foyer. Then along a sparkling, shining, white-painted corridor and into a sparkling, white-painted ward with windows along one side, overlooking the gardens. It was a large room with maybe fifty patients in two rows of simple, black-framed beds, and no frills at all. There Jack and Alec were allowed to climb into their beds and wait.

A nurse in white with a black skirt and a big, white apron over entered the ward frowning. Then she went to Alec. "Driver Alexander Morey?" she asked.

Alec nodded. "Yes."

"You seem to be over he worst of it, so we'll keep you on fluids for a few days and let nature take its course. Where are you bound for?"

"Training at Perham Downs."

"You'll be there in about a week."

"Thank you nurse."

The nurse wrote Alec's name on a small blackboard above his bed before going to Jack who was told the same thing and had his name written above his bed.

"Alec?" Jack asked after the nurse left.

"Yes Jack."

"Fourth Artillery Division can do without us for a week, don't you think?"

"I'm sure they can."

* * *

Australian soldiers were good at raiding; sneaking across no man's land to occupy a section of German trench, and then beating the enemy to death using their trench shovels and maybe taking a few prisoners. Major-General Monash obviously felt the same way because after some two months of minor raids, Monash locked himself away for a day to plan a big raid. And plan it he did, leaving nothing to chance including some weeks of training. The big raid was good for Martin because he had a chance to spend some time with their divisional commander beyond being just another headquarters lieutenant sharing mess at the dining table in the chateau. Some of the junior officers and many NCOs thought that Monash was aloof and distant, but Martin thought it was more likely that the General was uncomfortable with small talk unless he knew someone well. Working closely together, Martin found John Monash to be a decent man with clear ideas about what he wanted. He wanted the raid to be a success with minimal casualties, and he was convinced that thorough preparation would achieve that. The raid would start with an artillery barrage of gas shells to the German lines, only shortly before the raiders were due to cross no man's land, the gunners would switch to smoke shells. That meant German soldiers would be hampered by the bulk and poor visibility of gas masks which the Australians didn't have to wear. The Thirty-Seventh and Thirty-Eighth Battalions contributed just over 400 troops each, and the raiding party was put through two weeks of special training.

The date set for the big raid was the evening of 27th of February 1917, starting at twenty-two hundred hours. Major-General Monash went to the line in the evening to address the raiders in person, and Martin came along pretending he had signals work to do but really wanting to be a part of the action. He was impressed by Monash's manner of speaking; and especially the way he clearly and concisely summed up the scope and plan for the raid. He also reminded them of the torpedoing of the Lusitania and the murder of Nurse Cavell, which really got the men's blood up. Then Martin and Major-General Monash went to their battle headquarters in the basement of an abandoned shop in the devastated town of Armentières. Waiting were GSO1 Lieutenant-Colonel Jackson, GSO2 Major Wylly, Casualty Liaison Lieutenant Owen and two corporals from divisional administration. In the cold, stark room lit by a single bulb hanging on a wire, Martin sat in an old, timber chair in front of the switchboard on an old and scarred table. A light glowed and Martin connected the call through. He listened for a moment and hung up.

"The bombardment has started," he said while checking his watch and it was twenty-one thirty. At that moment the gunners would be firing gas shells before switching to smoke shells at twenty-one fifty. All was silence while they waited, with each minute taking an eternity. The light from Thirty-seventh battalion glowed and Martin connected the call and listened.

"The men are over the top," he said, and he tried to imagine what that would be like. The bombardment by German artillery, flares shot by the enemy illuminating men who didn't want to be seen, rifle fire, machine gun fire, shouts as they were killed before they reached the enemy wire, and cutting that wire without being trapped. He tried to picture what it was like to jump into the German front trench and beat grey-uniformed men to death with your shovel before they beat you to death with their shovels, and at the same time petrified that other grey-uniformed men further along the trench or in the secondary trench might realise what was going on and overpower you with sheer numbers and give you no chance for survival, but Martin was unable to do that either. All he could do was wait for news which could be good or bad or devastatingly bad.

The raid was timed for thirty minutes, with another five minutes to return across no man's land and report. If anything went wrong runners would relay the news if they could, and that would be phoned through to battle headquarters. No news was good news or, more likely, the runners couldn't get through. Still they waited in Armentières and Martin checked his watch for twenty-two twenty-five. The minutes dragged on and the light from Thirty-seventh battalion glowed and Martin answered the call from their signals officer, Alf Sanderson.

"The raiders have returned with seventeen prisoners," Martin said. "They're checking casualties now."

Alf rang through about ten minutes later with a count of ninety-eight wounded and ten missing presumed dead, for 100 to 200 enemy killed, although Martin wondered if every

German soldier the raiders met was killed. Maybe they were. Using shovels rather than rifles would have been a bloody business. Martin felt terrible that so many Australian soldiers had been killed and wounded, even though Monash had made it clear that Australian casualties were an inevitable part of war. Martin relayed that news to Major-General Monash and smiles broke out all round.

"Tell them that was well done," the Major-General said.

Martin relayed that message and asked for more details but none were available. "That's all the battalion has to report," he said.

The Major-General got up from his old, timber chair. "That was a worthwhile night," he said. "We gave the Hun something to think about. Thank you men and we can head back."

They left the cold, damp basement with Martin trailing.

"That went well," Major Wylly said.

"I believe it did sir," Martin replied, because it was expected that he would agree that the raid was good. Inwardly Martin felt that one Australian death or injury was one too many.

"You should take tomorrow off, and you too Harry."

"Thank you sir," Harry said.

From Armentières it was a thirty minute walk on duckboards and muddy roads to the chateau, by which time they both needed a bath and to clean their boots. But that could wait until the morning. Martin stripped to his underwear and fell into bed, but tossed and turned and found sleep difficult. He wondered if he was still keyed up over the raid, or affected by death and injury so close and yet so far away.

The following morning Martin washed his tunic and polished his boots while Harry went to check on the post. He returned about a half hour later carrying two parcels. "Here you go mate," he said."

Martin took them and sat on his bed. He opened the parcel from Veronica and inside were tins of dried fruit, tins of meat and vegetables, tins of evaporated milk, soap, toothpaste and the inevitable two pairs of knitted socks. And a letter telling him all about the important things she was doing for the war effort, and how it was important for Kevin, her husband, to keep the economy of the country going to support the war his way. He was a clerk at a bank. Martin put the parcel on his footlocker and opened the second parcel from The Red Cross. Inside were more tins of food, a pouch of tobacco and four pairs of socks.

"You get parcels all the time," Harry said.

"That's the advantage of having two older sisters to care for you," Martin said.

"I wouldn't know about having sisters."

"You have Edith and she sends you parcels."

Harry nodded in agreement. "What're you going to do with that lot?" he asked.

Martin eyed the pile his locker and the tinned food would make a nice change from rations, but the rest he had to eventually fit into his kit. And then he knew. "The men in the trenches need socks more than we do, so I'll take the socks and the tobacco to a mate in thirty-seventh battalion and he can hand them around."

"Good idea mate."

"I'll check on my tunic."

It wasn't yet dry, so it wasn't until early afternoon when they were ready to leave for Bailleul. That was a twenty minute walk on an icy cold day that seeped through gloves and scarves, and Martin wondered what to do once they got there. They'd been to a few cafes, seen the theatre a few times, and while it was always good to get away from the hut in the grounds of Chateau Steenwerck, there should have been more to his life on the front.

"I really need...," Harry said quietly, barely audible above the never-ending crump of artillery guns.

Martin glanced at his mate and then he understood. He didn't need what Harry needed, but he needed to hear a woman's voice and just hold her. "I agree."

In silence they passed through the square and along a street, and at a blue light, formerly a three-storey residence, Martin knocked on a door. The door eased open and was then opened all the way to reveal a middle-aged woman wearing an ornate, purple dress: long, flowing and in silk or satin. "Entre," she said and put out her hand, and Martin and Harry gave her their caps, gloves and scarves.

It was warm after the bitter cold outside, while muted lighting cast a pleasant glow in a building where all curtains were drawn. Floral wallpaper in the entry hall had seen better days, as had the red and gold striped wallpaper in a large sitting room to the right. There a cheerful fire crackled, and several young women in little more than their underwear lounged on red, velvet sofas. There were two British captains: one at a bar through the double doors in the adjacent dining room, and one in hushed conversation with a young woman in a short, black dress and black stockings.

"To stay with us will be thirty francs," the middle-aged woman said.

Martin nodded and opened his wallet to hand across three banknotes, and in return she gave him a brass token which Martin slipped into his pocket, and Harry also paid thirty francs and received a token.

"Would you like champagne, Monsieurs?" she asked.

"Yes please," Martin heard himself saying.

"Two francs."

Martin handed over two further banknotes and Harry did the same, and they were given tall, thin flutes already wet with condensation. Martin sipped the cool and bitter drink which was most refreshing.

A beautiful young woman barely covered by her short red dress got up from a sofa and drifted across the room. "Bonjour Monsieur," she murmured. "My name is Annette," she said in accented English.

"Bonjour Mademoiselle," Martin said. "Je m'apelle Martin."

"Vous parlez le Française."

"Oui."

She touched one of the badges on Martin's collar. "You are Australian," she said in French. "You are a long way from home."

Martin assumed there was a certain etiquette. "Would you like a drink?" he asked.

She nodded. "Yes please."

Martin handed over two francs to the barman and received a glass which he handed to Annette. She sipped her drink and Martin was transfixed by her plump, ruby red lips. She was divinely beautiful, from her delicate, slim face to her firm breasts, revealed by her short, red dress, and her long, slender, stockinged legs, also revealed by her short, red dress. "Come and we can talk for a while," she said.

She took Martin's hand and led him to a small sofa where Martin sat, and Annette sat very close with her leg rubbing his. "How long have you been in France?"

"Three months."

"It's a pity that war has brought you here. You would like my country when it's peaceful."

"Yes, I'm sure I would."

"Especially as you can speak French."

Martin nodded his head. He fell in love with her soft, sweet, feminine voice. It had been a long, long time. He sipped more champagne.

"Would you like another drink, or something else?"

Martin studied her beautiful face before letting his gaze drop lower. "Something else," he said quietly.

"The token, Monsieur."

Martin handed over the brass token which Annette slipped into her pocket. Then she gracefully stood; everything she did was smooth and graceful, and she took his hand and Martin stood. She led him past Harry conversing with a young woman in white, and they went to the hallway and up narrow stairs creaking with every footstep. Through a doorway into a small room only marginally bigger than the oversized bed it contained, and discreetly lit by a single, heavily shaded light in the ceiling. Martin put his near-empty glass on a table to the side of that bed and Annette came to him. He bent his head to kiss her, and he held her firm, fleshy buttocks in his big hands. He kissed her and held her and that was the best.

Annette eased away. "You should remove your uniform," she said, starting on the buttons of his tunic. She struggled with the thick material so Martin helped her, and soon his tunic was hung from a stand and his collarless shirt too, and then his boots were put neatly to one side and his breeches were hung in place. She returned from the stand near the door and Martin took her and hugged her again, and her body against the thin cotton of his underwear felt heavenly.

"I just want to hug you," Martin said. "Nothing more than that."

"I understand," Annette said. "But we should be naked because that will be better."

Martin removed his vest and underpants and Annette removed her small dress and her drawers. Martin gasped at her beauty when she turned around, and gasped again when she held him, her small hands resting on his buttocks, his big hands resting on her buttocks, his hardness pressed against her stomach. She reached down and wrapped her hand around his hardness and Martin gasped again.

"I want you to make love with me," she said.

Martin swallowed. "I can't make love to a woman I don't love."

She gripped him tighter. "I love you," she said before kissing him.

"I love you too."

She moved away and gracefully climbed onto the bed, and Martin gazed between her legs. She rolled onto her back and Martin lay above and kissed her, and lower and lower to her centre of femininity. He licked her and inhaled her sweet scent. Licked her and felt her and heard her and Martin had never made love that way before. He filled her while gazing into her beautiful brown eyes, and he made love with her. He made love with her while she hugged him, pulling him closer, and when he came he kissed the side of her neck while she held him tight.

"Tell me what it's like," she said softly.

"I work at a headquarters away from the lines, and there I'm mostly safe. But sometimes I have to go to the lines and sometimes I see terrible things. The artillery shells.... I feel guilty that I have a safe job."

"What do you do?"

"I keep communication open between the commander and his men."

"What would happen if you didn't do your job?"

Martin wondered, and knew what would happen with a big battle with so many elements to be coordinated. "It would be chaos," he said.

"Then you are saving thousands of men from death and injury by doing your job."

Martin thought about that and Annette was right. "Yes I am," he said. He lifted his head and looked into her eyes. "Tell me about you," he asked.

"I come from Lille, and when the Germans came they deported all healthy men to labour camps, including my father. My mother and I fled to the west and now I am here." She kissed his lips. "Make the Boche go away and give me back my country."

"How old are you?"

"Twenty. My real name is Marie."

"Why do you call yourself Annette?"

She smiled brightly. "Because no man wants to make love with a woman named Marie."

He kissed her. "I want to make love with a woman named Marie."

"Mon cheri; you can make love with me for the rest of the afternoon."

EIGHT

In early March Major-General Monash went away for two weeks leave. In the meantime the Germans started raiding Allied lines in Flanders and third division's role became more defensive. Shortly after the General returned, he went away for a meeting of divisional commanders. He came back with a plan to launch a major attack on Messines Ridge, and an extension of third division's lines to take in Ploegsteert Wood, a dismal patch of dead trees. The Germans held the high ground of the Messines Ridge to the south, and more ridges to the east of the city of Ypres. The front in Flanders was overlooked by German artillery on higher ground, and it was difficult to gain ground observation of the German rear areas east of those ridges. Despite that Martin was surprised that Field Marshal Haig proposed a major battle in Flanders. The war could never be won in the mud of Flanders.

While the extension of third division lines to Ploegsteert was undertaken, Martin made sure their lines of communication to the basement in Armentières were secure. That was an unfortunate part of his role, not because he could be a casualty but because he saw the death, destruction and misery that was an infantryman's way of life. Those nights in muddy, smelly trenches with the sound of artillery clear and distinct, he rarely slept.

The General travelled a lot by car and on horseback too, and at one stage he worked closely with Martin on his part of the grand plan called 'The Magnum Opus'. That became a particularly long day continuing after dinner, and Martin felt weary. When he rubbed his eyes out of tiredness he was excused for a half-hour to get some fresh air. Martin went to his hut to wash his face and drink a glass of water, and on the way back he paused at the top of the steps to Chateau Steenwerck. Martin leaned against the wall with his arms crossed and the silence was eerie. No artillery, no rifles, no shouts, no noise, no flares, nothing. There wasn't even a moon to illuminate the grounds. He absorbed the peace and quiet and, for the first time in a long time, felt glad to be alive.

Then Martin sensed movement and recognised the scent of boot polish and hair oil. The general came alongside and he leaned against the wall as well. He was the most unassuming man: medium build with a large nose, neatly-trimmed moustache, darkened skin and penetrating eyes that seemed not to miss a thing. But with his standard issue uniform and old and worn top boots, he might have been a signals lieutenant instead of commanding a division.

"All quiet on the Western Front," Martin said.

He sensed the general nodding in agreement. "How did you get here?" Major-General Monash asked.

Martin wondered how far to go before deciding that it could be his only opportunity. "I was raised in Brisbane where my parents died when I was thirteen. My older sisters looked after me, and later I won a scholarship to attend Brisbane Grammar to get my matriculation. I intended to go to university to study engineering...."

"Engineering?" Major-General Monash interrupted.

"Yes sir; I thought that would be a practical profession. Only I decided to take some time off first, and I arranged to inherit my parent's yacht while my sisters shared the house. I sailed the Esmeralda north to Cairns, and further north to Samarai in New Guinea. There I met a couple from The Red Cross who were looking for long-term transportation to coastal settlements and islands." Martin wondered if he should go further but he knew the general was agnostic, far from a prude, and once was a lady's man. "I also met someone and she became my...," and Martin didn't quite know the right word to use. And then he did. "Jara became my companion."

"She was from New Guinea?"

"She was." Martin would never forget that day they met. "She was beautiful in all ways," he said quietly. "We lived on the Esmeralda and Jara sailed with us. I already knew the basics of her language and she taught me more, and I taught her to handle the boat."

"Did you have children together?"

"No we didn't," Martin said, while knowing that the women of New Guinea had ways to avoid pregnancy when not married. "Then war broke out and living as I was in an Australian protectorate, I had to present for military training if not enlist; so I bid farewell to my tropical paradise. I sold the boat, travelled to Melbourne, and because of my matriculation they selected me to be a lieutenant."

"And now you are here."

"For now I'm here, but when this is over I'll go back."

"To live with your companion again?"

Martin thought about the ways of New Guinea. "We can learn many things from her people; how not to steal, how not to be jealous, how not to commit endless slaughter. But we can't learn how to wait for years and years for your sweetheart to return to you. They don't have that concept, but I can still go back to paradise."

"I don't know if I understand but I will take your word on these things."

"Tell me sir, how did you get here?"

"I was in the militia in Victoria for many years, and during that time I read many books on warfare, especially about the American civil war. While I was in Gallipoli I saw some successes and many failures, and I wanted to build on what I learned from that campaign. We must train our men well for their task in hand, for men in battle, rest and sleep are more important than anything else, we must have detailed plans clearly communicated to all participants so that the force is aimed and focussed on the prime objectives of the battle, and we must never change plans at the last moment."

Martin understood and especially the comment about rest and sleep. "You have a group of battalions taking the first objective, and a second group of battalions going past to take the next objective, which means you have fresher troops on the battle-front."

"Yes."

In the background heavy footsteps approached; all but stomping on the timber flooring.

"General...," Major Moore called from behind.

Monash sighed. "Duty calls. I'm glad we had this chat." He went inside.

Martin was glad they had that chat, but all it did was rekindle memories of a time that he once wished would last forever. He went inside while hoping his small contribution to The Magnum Opus would make a difference.

* * *

Mess in the dining room at the chateau was often a bright and happy place, where Major-General Monash enjoyed jokes in particular. But by any standards mess in the evening of April six was particularly jubilant and Martin wondered what happened. He sat at his place at the table and looked across at Monash.

"Have you heard the news?" Monash asked

"No sir," Martin said.

"The United States has declared war on Germany."

Martin was momentarily stunned, and then relieved. "That is good news sir. The surprise is that it took so long, with Americans killed when the Lusitania was torpedoed, and then the ongoing submarine blockade of the Atlantic."

"But that wasn't it. Germany was negotiating an alliance with Mexico, and the Americans found out."

Martin was even more stunned. "That was rather silly; Mexico has little to offer to the Central Powers."

"That's true enough."

"I wonder how long that will take to make a difference," Major Moore said.

Monash frowned. "They have to recruit their troops and officers, train them, send them to England, train them for the front and get them here."

"They will be raw when they get here," Martin said.

"They will be like Australians at Pozieres," Monash said.

"Yes."

Monash frowned. "Mid-next year in any numbers."

"We could lose before then," Major Moore said. "The Tsar has abdicated and the Bolsheviks have taken control of the Russian parliament."

"The Russian army has already mutinied," Monash said. "That means Germany can transfer troops from Russia to the Western Front."

"Do you know how many?"

"About a million I heard."

"Bloody hell!" Martin exclaimed.

"Absolutely right Lieutenant," Monash said. "And then the French...."

"What about the French sir?" Martin asked.

"Their troops have had enough of being used as machine gun targets. Just recently they went into battle baaing like sheep to the slaughter."

Martin nodded slowly while he thought about that. "That's not good."

"I heard that French troops are deserting at Chemin des Dames," Major Moore said.

"Today's a mix of good news and bad news," Martin said

"These circumstances put even more responsibility on the AIF to play its part in victory, and only by proper planning can we achieve that," Monash said. "Speaking of which I've got the Field-Marshal and the General visiting over the next few days. Please be on your best behaviour when they're around."

"We always are," Major Moore said.

"By Australian standards we are, but the British are sticklers for the rules."

And then the cooks brought out the meal with senior officers served first, and along the table in order of rank. Martin was pleased the Americans had joined the Allies, but the other news was troubling: a strengthened German army and a crippled French army.

In the meantime The Magnum Opus became bigger and ever more detailed, including objectives and procedures for each battalion, and in some cases employment of platoons and even sections. For the first time there was to be a substantial machine gun presence in an Allied battle, and that was long overdue. It was a new approach to warfare from a general who, maybe, benefitted from not having formal, military training, but rather relied on commonsense and intuition. At different times General Plumer and Field Marshal Haig visited and were briefed by Major-General Monash. It was rumoured they criticised

Monash for getting too much involved in detail, but Martin thought that it was time to change the way the war was waged. The previous year at the Somme was a tragedy for British and Empire forces; 60,000 casualties on the first day of battle and 400,000 casualties for the campaign, and if Monash's detailed plan worked then so much the better.

The battle was to be conducted by the Australian Third Division along with the British Twenty-fifth Division and the New Zealand Division, with the Australian Fourth Division kept in reserve. Headquarters staff were kept busy typing circular upon circular, while two massive and detailed scale models of the battlefield were constructed to help companies come to grips with the challenges facing them. Artillery guns of the fourth and third divisions, as well as the guns of British and New Zealand divisions were brought into position, and miners continued working deep underground.

On the 23rd of May the artillery barrage was increased in intensity, spotted by massive numbers of RFC aircraft who did their best to keep German aircraft at bay. Millions of shells had been stockpiled to damage the German lines, destroy their barbed wire and prevent enemy soldiers from sleeping. The noise and vibration in the hut in the grounds of Chateau Steenwerck was truly incredible; from morning to night an unrelenting onslaught against the German lines. Martin hoped, when he lay in bed at night, that the noise he heard was the first step towards a decisive victory.

Communications were planned and communications infrastructure was in place, so Martin had little to do until the day of battle. He played cards with Harry and played solitaire on his own, wrote letters to his sisters and went outside for walks just to get away for a few hours. But he couldn't get away from the noise of artillery, which carried many, many miles from the front.

Always at six in the evening they gathered in the mess, the dining room of the chateau, and always it was cheerful but much less so on the 27th. Martin sat beside Harry; his place in the order of rank.

"Have you heard the news?" Harry asked quietly.

Martin shook his head. "No," he said.

"Rumour has it that the French army has suffered widespread mutiny."

Martin was shocked, and his expression must have shown.

"You heard what's happening?" Major Moore asked.

"I did sir," Martin replied.

"There's a rumour that some or perhaps many French enlisted men went to the rear of their lines at Aisne, and refused to take further part in the war. But we don't know for certain, so it's essential that this rumour be kept secret. "

"I understand sir."

"And the enemy must never hear about this rumour."

"Of course sir," Martin said, understanding the implications.

While the French Armée de Terre might or might not have been having problems at Aisne, the artillery barrage continued in Flanders, Allied air superiority played its part, and Martin was sure that extra machine guns would make a difference. He lay in his bed hoping the noise he heard would help the Allies in their noble but invariably futile quest to take Messines Ridge. He was certain the war could never be won in Flanders.

* * *

Alec gazed out of the doorway of the train in wonder. Soldiers everywhere, coming and going, and in the midst of the chaos their train pulled into the station at Steenwerck. For many hours he heard the guns booming, and the further they travelled the louder the sound of artillery until it seemed as if the freight truck was shaking with the noise. Waiting on the platform were several double-decker stretcher carts with seemingly lifeless shapes partly covered by army blankets. The wounded to be taken away for treatment; a sobering sight. The train lurched to a stop and the replacement troops climbed down to the low-set platform, opposite a large but plain brick station building with a veranda.

The station was chaotic until an Australian sergeant with a loud hailer called for the replacement gunners and drivers for the Fourth Field Artillery Division, and they loosely formed into order at the far end of the platform. The sergeant pulled a notebook out of his pocket and read out names, and all answered in turn while the sergeant ticked his list. He then asked them to follow him and filed off the platform and onto a dusty track. A large group of men approached, and the new arrivals had to move to one side to let them by. There were hundreds of German soldiers, Alec recognised their spiked helmets from pictures in the newspapers, and they were escorted or guarded by a dozen NCOs and infantrymen. Close up they didn't look like the enemy at all. Many were young, not even twenty, and their eyes darted left and right and even at the newly-arrived gunners and drivers. They were just ordinary, young men in grey uniforms and grey helmets with spikes on top.

The sergeant returned to the track, and Alec continued walking amongst the many Australian soldiers passing to and fro.

"What do you think of this?" Jack asked Alec.

"Something big's happening or maybe the front lines are always like this," Alec said. He really didn't know.

They rounded a corner and came to a long, low barn in grubby, whitewashed brick, where all was surrounded by dry dust and dirt. A few hardy trees added a little greenery to the mostly bleak sight. The whole area: tents to the left, the barn to the right, the open ground in the middle was bustling with hundreds of men in the khaki of the AIF. Behind the barn and further away in paddocks fenced by timber railings were hundreds of horses of the AIF.

"My name's David Else," the sergeant said. "Gunners will come with me to the line while drivers are billeted here at the barn, and your horses are out the back. Driver John Davies is allocated to forty-sixth battery, Driver Alexander Morey to forty-seventh, Driver Bert Murray to forty-fifth battery and Driver Arthur Wood also to forty-fifth. Get comfortable for now, and dinner's about six over there," he said, pointing in the direction of two tents with dark, camouflaged rooves. "Have a good night's sleep, breakfast's at five, and I'll be back at six tomorrow morning. Gunners, you have an early start tomorrow at three."

Alec checked his watch and it was half-past five, so he had half an hour before some inevitably unpalatable army rations. He went past the open double timber doors into the barn, slipped his kit off his shoulders and got as comfortable as he could on some coarse, prickly straw piled to one side.

He pulled out his part-finished letter to Dorothy and wrote about his arrival at the front. Eventually he would mail that letter while knowing that it would take the best part of three months to get to her, by which time anything could have happened. He looked towards a queue forming at the mess tent, so he took his bowl and utensils and fell into line. Cooks stripped to the waist on account of the hot, June weather and their exertions, ladled stew and other cooks ladled tea, and Alec returned to the barn to eat his meal. He sat next to Bert: young, tall, lanky and enthusiastic. Alec got to know Bert during their travels.

"Been writing to Dorothy?" Bert asked.

"Yes I have," Alec said.

Bert nodded thoughtfully; he was only 19 and he didn't have a wife or fiancee. Alec was fatigued after travel by train from the camp to Southampton, then by ferry across the channel to Boulogne where they camped for a few days, and then the best part of a day in a train crossing northern France. He never, every thought he would visit France.

The evening drifted lazily and Alec thought it would be useful to have a book to pass the time, even though he wasn't a big reader, but all he could carry was that which fitted into his kit. He laid his greatcoat out as a bed on the coarse straw, and he lay on his back and hoped that sleep would come.

* * *

Martin sat in front of the switchboard with a wireless set to his right, tuned to the frequency to be used by the aircraft observers. He checked his watch and the second hand crept closer and closer to three-ten. And then the explosions were felt as much as heard when 21 mines deep below the German front line were detonated. In the basement dust swirled, the brick and concrete walls swayed for several moments while the light globe swung wildly. What was the effect on the enemy? Hundreds, no thousands were obliterated, and what remained of their front lines after weeks of intensive shelling would have been flattened. Surely that would have more than made up for the unfortunate gas attack on the Australian Third Division the evening before. The mine explosions would be followed by artillery batteries firing a creeping barrage in three belts 700 yards deep, while the designated counter-battery artillery groups bombarded all known German artillery positions with gas shell, and the thunder of that barrage could be heard and felt in the cold basement in Armentières. The nine attacking divisions assisted by tanks would begin their advance across no man's land against an enemy weakened and disorientated. The telephone rang from the Thirty-seventh Battalion reporting that Germany artillery had shelled the assembly trenches, but too late.

Martin knew that for the third division infantry, the training of Monash's big mine explosion exercise at Lark Hill would make for a major advantage when the time came to consolidate mine craters. And so it seemed with near-continual wireless reports of their infantry advancing on all fronts against little resistance. An advance protected by the creeping bombardment and also protected by those artillery batteries tasked with the job of silencing enemy artillery. All the time allied machine guns fired over the heads of the advancing troops, raining lead against the enemy and keeping them pinned behind what remained of their trench breastworks.

The telephone hardly rang and all the observations came by wireless from the aircraft observers. The initial advance took and held the blue line and Field Artillery were then instructed to pause the bombardment until four-thirty, as planned. That was to allow fresh battalions to move forward to take the black line, further into enemy-held territory. Second Army Headquarters telephoned that the New Zealanders took the village of Messines, and Martin reported that the Australian Third Division took all Stage One objectives.

* * *

The following morning saw an early breakfast at the mess tents: tea and army biscuits, and Alec was glad for the mug of tea to soak and soften biscuits as hard as small bricks. David Else came into the barn and did a headcount of his drivers.

"Right men," David said. "There's a battle underway today, has been since three-ten, and today we're bringing shells to the line." The drivers were taken out the back where horses munched on the last of the grass in the smallest paddock. The drivers were allocated to work as pairs for each battery: Alec with Tom Wheeler of forty-seventh battery. Tom was a country boy from near Bendigo: tall, strapping and easy going, and he knew his horses too. Each pair of drivers hitched two horses to a cart, and once ready Tom and Alec climbed onto their cart.

Tom called the horses and they got away. "G'day Alec," he said while he got comfortable. "First day on the front?"

"Yes it is," Alec said. "How long have you been here, Tom?" he asked.

"Two months, but only over the last two weeks has it been busy like this. Most of the time we groomed the horses and waited for something to do."

Alec was surprised to hear that.

"It'll be good to work together mate," Tom said.

"It will be," Alec said.

Tom drove their cart along a dusty track lined by dead trees, towards where it was busier further along. Alec spotted a massive ammunition dump with thousands or maybe hundreds of thousands of shells stacked beneath camouflage netting, partially peeled back to allow access to shells at one end. The drivers loaded their carts and Alec got hotter and hotter until he removed his tunic. Working in just his collarless shirt was much better, and eventually their cart was loaded with about two hundred shells. They climbed on board and Tom drove towards the noise of guns firing close by, maybe a thousand yards away or so, and once they crossed a low ridge Alec saw the batteries working hard. For a moment he wished he was a gunner and not a driver. He knew how to operate a gun, he was one of the best in training, and he was wasted loading carts with ammunition. They pulled up at forty-seventh battery and unloaded and stacked their shells. Alec noticed that Jack was aiming the gun, so he was allocated to the same battery.

Without a word being said and bare acknowledgement of their presence, Alec and Tom climbed onto their cart for the return journey to the ammunition dump. There they started loading and Alec knew it was going to be a long, hot day.

* * *

The battle paused at eleven to deal with an expected German resistance, with the enemy expected to re-group. In the meantime artillery was to be brought forward into no man's land and more tanks were brought forward for the next stage of the battle, planned to be begin at thirteen hundred hours. Second Army Headquarters then telephoned to inform Major-General Monash that the next stage was delayed because the British divisions were not yet in place, and Martin was ordered to ring every Brigade and Battalion of fourth division and tell them to hold their troops. He was able to get through and near-disaster was avoided, and then it became a case of waiting and hoping that the British delay didn't ruin what had turned into a successful battle. Eventually Second Army Headquarters rang through just before fourteen twenty-five with a new start time of fifteen hundred hours, and Martin had a busy time to ensure that all Brigades and Battalions were confirmed ready to go. From there the wireless observations resumed, the men on the ground obviously not using runners, and the news was good. Fourth division was able to pass through the newly consolidated front lines and take the green line. The battle was a success.

* * *

All changed into chaos. A lieutenant at the ammunition dump told the drivers that horses and carts were to be taken to the barn, and then all guns were to be moved into what was no man's land. The drivers of forty-seventh battery: Henry, Joe, Tom and Alec hitched a team of six, fresh horses to the drawgear for an eighteen pounder, and Joe and Tom then mounted two of those horses. Escorted by Henry and Alec they rode the drawgear across the dry, dusty ground heading towards their gun. When they arrived the horses were ridden in a semi-circle to bring the drawgear close to the gun's pole trail, and the gunners sweated, grunted and swore with the exertion of lifting and carrying the gun and slotting it into place. Once secure they did another semi-circle and headed towards the trenches in the near distance.

Alec expected trenches to be trenches, but they were walls of sandbags partially demolished to allow the guns to get through. There were several rows of trenches, empty and abandoned given the new front line somewhere to the east, and they rode their gun past those trenches and onto ground more devastated that Alec could ever imagine. Progress slowed while they dodged as many shell craters as possible, but it wasn't always possible and the horses had to be whipped hard to pull the gun out of craters in the way. They rode close to David Else and rode the horses around in a semi-circle to have the gun facing in the right direction. Again the gunners strained and swore while they unhitched their weapon and rolled it onto more even ground. Other batteries also brought their guns into place while the drivers of forty-seventh rode the horses and drawgear back to the billet, and then hitched up carts for the next part of the exercise: bringing shells into place.

It took an hour to ride their carts to the old gunnery position, load two hundred shells each, ride to the gun and unload with the gunner's assistance. And then back for more shells, and when they unloaded the gun was in use and firing. Alec and Tom were busy unloading when Alec sensed something strange. He turned around to see what it was when a shell burst about 50 yards short of the batteries with the most massive explosion, and sprayed dirt high into the air. Another shell then came in about 50 yards short, and they were under fire from the Huns! All the time the corporal called the range through his megaphone, the gunners worked without a pause while Tom and Alec unloaded and stacked shells. They emptied the cart, climbed on board and rode away and Alec sensed yet another shell but very close and he turned to see it, and some gunners ducked while others threw themselves onto the ground for protection. Alec watched as they got up except for Charlie, who held his chest with his uniform changing colour with his blood. Alec jumped from the cart and ran to Charlie surrounded by the men of his battery, and suddenly felt faint at the sight of his injuries: his chest torn open, his insides visible and blood everywhere.

"Stretcher bearers!" the Corporal boomed through his loudhailer above the noise of batteries still firing. Alec felt useless just standing there and he looked towards the corporal.

"Alec, there's nothing you can do," he said.

"Yes, alright," Alec mumbled and he walked to the cart in a daze. He climbed on while Henry and Joe came into view with their cart laden with shells. Tom called the horses and they rolled away past the craters, dodging as many as they could but struggling with those which were impossible to dodge, until they reached the flatter ground of the old trenches.

"That was bad luck for Charlie," Tom eventually said.

Alec sighed. "Yes, that was bad lack for Charlie. I don't think he'll make it."

"I hope they get morphine to him at least."

"Do the stretcher bearers carry morphine?"

"They do."

"That's good to know."

Alec didn't know Charlie at all well, gunners slept at their guns and drivers slept in the barn near their horses, but to see anyone with those injuries was truly, truly stomach-churning.

Alec and Tom loaded more shells, and when they returned the men at the gun were struggling a crew of five.

Alec and Tom unloaded their shells until David Else came to them.

"You're both trained as gunners," he said. "Who wants to take over?"

"I can," Alec said. "I did extra militia training as a gunner."

David nodded in acknowledgement. "Righto mate, you do that. Tom, just do what you can alone."

"Alright Dave," Tom said.

Tom climbed onto his cart while Alec grabbed his tunic and draped it over the pile of shells. He put his protective wax in his ears, went to the crew, grabbed a shell and handed it to George who handed it to Jack who fed it into the breach. Bill was on the trigger, Frank aiming while Bob dealt with the used casings. They worked like that for a while before swapping over, with Alec feeding shells into the breach. And so the afternoon went on with the corporal calling changes in range through his megaphone. Very busy but very mechanical, and too much time to remember Charlie's injuries. Alec knew Charlie wouldn't make it, but he hoped his last moments weren't too painful.

* * *

The information coming into battle headquarters showed the advance was slowing and the battle for the final objective, the Oosttaverne line, had much harder fighting from what the aircraft observers reported. Sections of the Oosttaverne line were taken while resistance was harder in others, until the battle petered out later in the evening with the greatest success ever achieved by the Allies on the Western Front. The objective for day one, the green line, was taken in less than twelve hours. Martin began to think that the war could be won in Flanders after all.

He should have been tired after such a long day, three in the morning until after ten in the evening, but the excitement of being part of such a great victory prevented sleep. Instead he lay in his bed and considered the implications of what happened.

"Harry?" he called.

"Yeah mate," was the tired response.

"This was the first big victory for the AIF."

"It was."

"Do you think they will remember this?"

"I hope they remember this. It's better to remember a great victory instead of glorious but futile defeat."

"You mean Gallipoli?"

"I do. Today we had the Hun on the run, and who would have thought that day would ever come. Let's hope the rest of the battle goes as well."

Martin hoped what remained, the taking of the Oosttaverne line, would go well. But the Germans had time to organise themselves and those last hundreds of yards would be hard going. He wondered just how hard it was going to be.

* * *

They flopped on the ground in the darkness; too tired to move. Alec sat with his back to the wheel of the gun; he'd never been so exhausted in all his days. Then he sensed something and looked up to see David Else.

"Thanks for helping out today," David said.

"That's alright," Alec said.

"You can stay here for the while; get your kit from the barn."

"I will. How was Charlie?"

"He didn't make it."

"That's too bad." Alec didn't want to ask on the back of another man's misfortune, but if it wasn't to his advantage then it was to the advantage of the battery. "I can take his place if you want."

"Thanks Alec. I'll speak to John and get you transferred across."

"Who's John?"

"Lieutenant Black. We'll get you re-mustered as gunner and this'll be your new home."

"How did the battle go?"

"Alright from what I heard. They took most of Messines Ridge."

"That's good isn't it?"

"It's about time we had some good news. But the battle's not over 'till it's over and I'm sure the Hun will be making life tough for our blokes over there, so remember them."

"Don't worry David," Alec said. "We know the war can't be won without artillery." Alec grabbed a spoke of the dirty, green wheel and lifted himself up. "I must get my kit."

Alec trudged away in the general direction of Steenwerck, and there was more to his walk than getting his things. He had to say goodbye to Tom, Joe and Henry.

NINE

Martin and Harry walked along dusty roads towards Bailleul
as part of seven days away from the front for the entire
division, and seven days away from the chateau for non-
essential headquarters staff. It had taken seven, long days
and many tens of thousands of killed and wounded to take
and consolidate the Oosttaverne line. Preliminary figures
showed about 26,000 casualties in total: more than 3,000
casualties for the Third Australian Division, almost 3,000
casualties for the Fourth Australian Division and about 5,000
casualties for the New Zealand Division. Major-General
Monash conducted a thorough debriefing after the battle,
determined to learn from any failures as well as successes.
After that they had a well-deserved break although Martin
wondered he was going to do in Bailleul for seven days.

German artillery boomed out and explosions could be
heard quite close by. Martin wondered what the Germans
were shelling, but at least they weren't shelling the road to
Bailleul. Martin and Harry closed on that town where all was
chaos, and Martin discovered the Germans were shelling
the little town of Nieppe; part-way to the front line. Major
Moore ran up from the chateau and intercepted Harry and

then Martin. "General Monash wants us to help in Nieppe," he said.

"Of course," Harry said.

"We need to evacuate civilians and fight some fires which have broken out."

"Right away sir."

"We'll get rid of our kits and be there in a moment," Martin said.

Martin led the way to their billet on Rue de la Gare to dump their bulky kits, and then they ran towards Nieppe which was to the north of the chateau. By the time they reached the small town of red brick buildings, some of the enlisted men were unrolling fire hoses while others were escorting women, children and the elderly out of their homes. Shells rained down and some exploded in the town, causing terrible damage to streets and buildings. Martin was sickened that the Germans would do that to defenceless citizens. Many terrible things had been said about the Huns, and on that day they proved to be true. Bailleul was safe and out of range, so Martin instructed two NCOs to escort the poor, stunned inhabitants of Nieppe to the Bailleul town square. Once safe they could make whatever arrangements were necessary, and Martin thought the town hall would be suitable for the night. There were not so many people remaining in Nieppe so it didn't take long to get them onto the road and out of harm's way, but it was necessary to search each and every habitable home just in case. They found some more and escorted them to Bailleul, and when Martin reached the square he saw about 200 poor, miserable wretches. The good natured folk of Bailleul pitched in and took the refugees into their own homes, while in the background the artillery barrage had stopped. All that remained was to extinguish the fires and hopefully the majority could return to their homes the next morning.

Martin returned to Nieppe and third division infantry were dealing with four fires. Some homes had been damaged but not so many, so most of the refugees had somewhere to live when the situation was under control. Martin was also impressed with the initiative shown by the Australian infantrymen. They were not fire fighters but they did it regardless, and very effectively from what Martin saw. He felt proud to call himself an Australian. After a long night the fires were eventually extinguished, and Martin returned to his billet to grab a couple of hours rest. It had been an eventful few hours.

He rose later in the morning to have breakfast with Monsieur and Madame Collin, Harry then appeared a few minutes later and greeted their hosts before sitting at the table. Madame Collin went to the bench to slice bread and boil water for their coffee.

"Bloody Huns," Harry mumbled.

Martin agreed with that sentiment. "There isn't a man in this war who hasn't sacrificed a lot to be here," Martin said. "That atrocity yesterday reminded me of why I did it."

"That's right. You gave up a lot."

"Wouldn't you rather be at home with Edith?"

"Not while the Huns do things like that."

"Nobody died and few buildings were destroyed, so it wasn't as bad as it could have been."

"But why do things like that?"

Martin didn't know.

After fresh, crusty bread and coffee they returned to Nieppe where the majority of the citizens had returned to their homes, and fortunately the majority of their homes were inhabitable with only one family left without lodgings. There wasn't anything Martin could do about that so they returned to Bailleul, and on the way Martin wondered what he could do there. The blue light and Marie were available but Martin thought not. Their time together had been good and he really needed the touch of a woman, but it was false and any man with enough money could buy pretend intimacy from a beautiful, young woman. And then he spotted someone familiar, but in uniform. Martin left Harry and went to the figure and then alongside. "Louis!" he exclaimed.

"Martin!" Louis exclaimed equally surprised. "Good to see you."

"Good to see you too. Where are you posted?"

"The casualty clearing station at Steenwerck."

"I'm at Chateau Steenwerck."

"Chateau?"

"It's divisional headquarters and we have a hut in the grounds."

Harry came alongside. "Lieutenant Harry Owen, this is my friend from New Guinea, Lieutenant and Dr Louis Middleton."

"Pleased to meet you Louis," Harry said, putting out his hand to shake.

"Please to meet you Harry," Louis said while shaking hands.

Martin glanced at his watch, and with all the running about it was almost midday. "What are you doing here in Bailleul?" he asked Louis.

"Three days off," Louis said. "This is my last day. And you?"

"We've seven days off but are up to day two already. Do you want to have lunch? I know a nice cafe"

"Of course, yes."

Martin led the way. "How's Sarah?" he asked.

"She was good in her last letter. We're parents now. Albert Louis."

"Congratulations."

They reached the cafe and went inside. The waitress showed them to a table for four, with a number of other tables taken. She returned with three menus.

"They do a good stew," Harry said.

Martin nodded while smiling brightly. The waitress returned and she was given orders for three of the potée Lorraine, two glasses of red wine and a glass of beer.

"How was Jara when you left her?" Martin asked.

"She was radiant," Louis said. "As all mothers to be are radiant."

"She has a good husband?"

"I think so."

"I'm glad," Martin said, and he meant that too. "I'm going back when this is over."

"New Guinea's a beautiful country of gentle, lovely people. We would go back but it's not a place for European children."

Martin understood; schooling in Samarai was poor and the only option would be to send a child to boarding school. And that would be difficult because any European child raised in New Guinea would have difficulties assimilating. All in all it wasn't a place for European children.

"You could have a relationship," Louis said. "Melanesian women like white men. You're more self-sufficient if that's the right word."

Martin knew that was true, although he doubted if he could re-create the magic he enjoyed with Jara. But even without that magic, life in Samarai would be much better than dull, boring Brisbane. "Yes I could," Martin said.

"Many Australian men in New Guinea have relationships with Melanesian women, and invariably they're very happy together."

"Melanesian women are calm and placid by nature, but underneath that they know what they want."

"Women form the backbone of their domestic and tribal life."

"That's true. Men do the hunting, fishing and wage wars, and women keep everything else together."

"They're often very beautiful."

Martin nodded while remembering.

"I liked being a small part of your world while we sailed together," Louis said.

"I liked having good company on our voyages," Martin replied.

"I'll always remember our time in New Guinea as the happiest time of my life. Unfortunately...."

Martin understood, now that they were parents.

"I feel like I've missed out on something," Harry said.

"You know what we're talking about?" Martin asked.

"Yes I do."

"I'm going back as soon as this is over."

Their drinks and food arrived, stifling conversation for a while.

"How's your posting going?" Martin asked Louis.

Louis sighed. "I am glad I enlisted to help, but I see the worst side of this terrible war. The men are often cheerful despite appalling injuries, and that rips at my heart. The ones in the front lines are worse, sometimes we get gunners and drivers gassed or shelled, and we get a lot of disease as you would expect from the conditions they live under. And other diseases of course."

"Of course," Martin said while deciding to take no more risks with Marie, and hoping she wouldn't be inflicted one day. Make the Boche go away she said, and he really wanted to do that for her.

"This war can't last forever," Louis said.

"I just want it to be over so I can go home," Martin said.

"Me too."

They finished their drinks and Martin didn't know what should follow.

"What're you thinking of?" Harry asked.

Then it hit Martin. "We've still got five days, so let's go to Paris."

"That sounds like a great idea," Louis said. "I've got to get back to my billet which isn't a chateau, so I'll leave you two to enjoy your sightseeing.

They all stood and shook hands. "It's been good to meet like this," Martin said.

"Pleased to meet you," Harry said.

"You two do your best to win this war and end the slaughter," Louis said.

They went outside and Louis walked alone towards Steenwerck. Martin headed to the left towards the station to catch a train to Paris.

* * *

Over time Alec got to know his mates on battery forty-seven. He met Jack Walsh on the Borda and they shared dysentery together. Jack was 21 and unable to enlist earlier, because his father had cleared off and his mother wouldn't sign his forms because she wanted the money he earned. Jack was a similar height to Alec but with black hair and dark eyes, and worked here and there as he put it, but wouldn't be more specific than that. Bob Brown was a former school teacher from Ballarat, older at 24 and married with two children. Tall and slender with brown hair and brown eyes; he seemed like a school teacher, studious and always thinking, and not at all like a gunner. Tall and gangly George Bool was 19 and single, and once worked as a baker before reading about the terrible casualties and deciding that his country really needed him. Frank Dickson was a small, muscular man with the strength of two or three ordinary blokes. Formerly working on the docks that was no surprise. Frank was older at 26 and married, and he looked for adventure and to get away from his missus as he put it. Chubby redhead Bill Smith was an apprenticed fitter and turner aged 21, and like Alec he couldn't enlist until he finished his apprenticeship. Like Alec, Bill was engaged; his sweetheart was Amy, and he looked forward to winning the war and getting home to get married. Overseeing the battery and five others was Corporal Paul Allen, Paul, who was a loner who kept his distance.

After more than three weeks at the front, the men of Fourth Field Artillery Division were sent away for a two week's rest at Bailleul nearby. After two hours' walk while singing songs, they arrived at a farm about a mile beyond the busy little town. It seemed that the drivers had exchanged accommodation at one barn for accommodation at another, although the new barn was surrounded by green grass and many, lush trees. But first a bath beckoned, and big open vats waited with the promise of a hot bath given the water boiling nearby. It was only lukewarm but that didn't matter; especially in the heat of late June. After, they were given 'new' uniforms which were anything but new, but at least cleaned. Then followed dinner from mess tents pitched to one side: army rations and a mug of tea. After that they had the rest of the night free at Bailleul. They gathered into groups, battery gunners with battery gunners and battery drivers with battery drivers, and headed into the town.

"Alec, what are you going to do?" Jack asked.

"Take a look around and maybe have a drink," Alec said, given that it'd been a long time. Not that he drank much, having turned 21 the day enlisted, and he only had a few glasses of beer when on leave from Maribyrnong and also when on leave from Perham Downs. But after a long time working hard, a glass of French beer seemed like a good way to spend leave in France.

They approached the busy, bustling town seemingly a world away from trenches and artillery, and not so far away given there were hundreds of soldiers from all the countries of the Empire.

"There are a lot of Poms here," Jack said.

"There are," Alec agreed.

"You know they only get sixpence a day."

Alec was surprised. "That's not much."

"That leaves the best for us."

Alec nodded in agreement. Bailleul was a town of small and old multi-storey houses and shops crowding narrow footpaths of narrow streets. A bit like the towns in England which had small and old homes all squashed together, such as the little town at Perham Down. At one of the buildings, a building with a red light, a queue formed.

"Alec, do you want to?" Jack asked.

Alec glanced at his mate. "No thanks Jack."

"Go on! You don't know what might happen and it might be your last chance. Look at Charlie...."

Alec thought a brothel was wrong no matter what happened to poor Charlie, and that was that. But whatever Jack did was his own business. "You go and you can tell me all about it, and if it's good I will go."

"Are you sure?"

"I'm sure."

"Catch you in town later," Jack said, and he went to the queue of about eight or nine men. Alec trailed the others and they reached a large, cobbled square with a big building on one side, looking like a church but with clocks instead of a steeple, and all around were shops and cafes and one that looked promising. Some of the cafes were small and posh and better suited to officers, while that cafe was big, rambling and had many simple, long, timber tables each surrounded by simple timber chairs. Alec led the way inside and it was bustling, boisterous, smoky and very, very busy. Alec had to muscle his way to the bar which as always wasn't easy because he wasn't particularly tall, although the Poms were mostly about his height and build. A rough-hewn woman with a few missing teeth, maybe in her forties or maybe older, came to serve him.

"A beer please," Alec asked.

"One franc and fifty centimes," she said in an accented voice.

Alec gave her a note and a coin and received a big, pint glass of cold beer pulled from a tap.

"Let's find a table," Bill said, and there were spaces at the end of a table of Canadians.

"Where you from?" one of the Canadians asked in their strange, nasally, drawling accent.

"Australian gunners," Alec said.

"Welcome to Bailleul."

"Thank you."

Suddenly there was a terrible ruckus and Alec couldn't see what happened. And then he did; two drunken Poms bumped into some Australians and were dealt with. Amongst other things Alec heard 'you spilt my beer you drunken, Pommy bastard!'. There was a bit of pushing and shoving but no punches were thrown, and for a moment Alec wondered why he was there. What was the point of being in a crowded bar full of drunken soldiers, and drinking beer which he didn't particularly like?

"What're you thinkin' about," the Canadian asked.

"What's the point to life on the front?" Alec said.

"To survive until your time's up."

Alec sipped his beer and wondered if Jack had the right idea after all. The next casualty could be him and time wasn't for wasting. But he was engaged and brothels were wrong, although Jack was engaged and that was just as bad. He should have stayed at the billet and done something useful like write a letter to Dorothy or to his mother. Alec sighed; he would do that tomorrow. He was stuck in Bailleul with the men of his battery and he couldn't leave them for seeming like a spoilsport, so he was stuck with it.

"Want another beer?" Bill asked.

Alec shook his head. "No thanks Bill."

Bill came back with his pint refilled and a paper in his hand, and Alec wondered how he managed to drink so much.

"What's that you got?" Frank asked.

"'The Wipers Times' it says. There's an advertisement here. 'Are you a victim of optimism? Do you wake in the morning feeling that all is going well for the Allies and believing our leaders are competent to conduct the war to a successful conclusion? The cure for this unhealthy optimism is two days in our establishment, and this will effectually eradicate all traces of optimism from your system'."

"Those Pommies are mad bastards," Frank grumbled.

"They're right," Bob said. "We spent so effort much taking a ridge, what, two miles from where we were? And how many would have died to take those miles? How many will die to push Germany all the miles out of France? More than what we've got I tell you."

"They ought to make you a general."

"I don't know what the answer is, but killing Charlie and thousands like him just to take two miles isn't going to win this war."

Alec had never heard such talk before, but in a way Bob was right.

"What about Gallipoli?" Bob asked. "What a fuck-up that was!"

"Yeah right," were the universal agreement.

"I reckon we ought to have another round," Bill said. "And you too Alec!"

Alec handed over his glass to be refilled, and in an alcohol-blurred haze the gunners of forty-seventh battery, except Jack who was otherwise engaged, worked out a strategy to win the war.

* * *

Alec woke with a pounding headache and feeling dreadfully thirsty. He grabbed his canteen and the water slaked his thirst. He felt queasy and decided to skip breakfast. His mates stirred and the pots boiled nearby: big closed pots with built-in burners beneath. Alec went to a cook and got his mug filled with tea but skipped on the biscuits. He returned to the barn and got comfortable, more or less.

"How did it go last night?" Jack asked Alec.

"We went to a cafe and had a few beers," Alec said. He hoped he wasn't going to hear more about Jack's night but guessed that was inevitable.

"I wouldn't bother with the red lights if I was you," Jack said. "They had a house with seven or eight rooms, and I got a woman old enough to be my mum on a camp bed with a rumpled sheet, and ten minutes."

Alec nearly choked on his tea and he looked at Jack with his eyes wide. That was terrible, and worse for the poor woman involved. Much worse for all the poor women in all of those places.

"Bloody officers get blue lights," Jack grumbled. "I don't reckon they get a camp bed and ten minutes."

"We're not officers; we're gunners."

"I know mate. Maybe we could sneak in."

"Our uniforms will give us away."

"The officers won't mind sharing...."

"I think they would, especially the Pommy officers from what I can see."

"I suppose you're right." Jack looked over to where it was busy. "I'll get some tea."

"How're you lot this morning?" Paul Allen asked. 'I've got good news. Major-General Holmes is coming tomorrow and we're to form up on parade."

There were grumbles and protestations that they were on leave, but Paul wouldn't have any of that. "I want your buttons polished, your boots polished; even your mess tins polished."

"You joking," Jack growled after he returned carrying his battered mug which looked like it defied polishing.

"I'm not."

"The least you can do is give us the day off after."

"I'll see what I can do."

Alec polished the buttons on his 'new' old uniform and polished his boots too, and they came up well. He even polished his mess bowl and mug, and once spick and span he set to writing to Ruby his oldest sister, eleven years older than he. Alec wrote about his time on the front, mentioning that he became a gunner when one of the men was unfortunately killed, but left out the details of poor Charlie's terrible injuries of course. He then wrote to Bessie his second sister, seven years older, and recounted the same details. Alec sighed and turned over the page of his notebook to write to his parents. Alfred Morey was 40 when they had Alec and his mother Helen was 37; ages not common to be having children but not uncommon either. He repeated the same stories except the death of Charlie. He didn't want to upset his mother. He finished by addressing three envelopes and hoped he could post his letters when he next went to Bailleul.

The following day they were put through parade ground manoeuvres for the benefit of several senior officers including Major-General Holmes with the neat moustache, and later Major-General Holmes congratulated them on the fine work they did during the battle of Messines. They were even told they did the AIF proud. The day after that was free in Bailleul, and Alec mailed his letters and took in the sights of the church and other fine, old and attractive buildings. Then he had a nice stew and a cup of coffee at a small cafe that seemed popular with Australian officers. The next day was cricket for enlisted men against officers, and

Alec immediately volunteered to open for his team and he put two bob on the enlisted men to win. The enlisted men won the toss and Alec scored a quick 52 before edging a ball to the 'keeper. He was applauded when he left the impromptu oval, but he was annoyed to lose his concentration on reaching his half-century. A simple mistake, and he was still annoyed when he went to get a mug of tea.

"Where'd you learn to play like that?" Jack asked while Alec returned with his drink.

"I play for Brighton seconds," Alec said. "I scored a century opening partnership in the thirds when I was fourteen."

"Get away!"

Alec shrugged his shoulders and momentarily remembered that newspaper article: the veteran and the colt.

The officers had no answer in the afternoon and the enlisted men won quite comfortably. Alec made four shillings given the odds were against his team.

"You know you won the game for your team," Tom said when he paid out.

"I know," Alec said, having gotten over his annoyance. Cricket had been a big part of his life for many, many years. He looked forward to when the war was over and returning to Brighton. Some said he might have a future at State level and play for Victoria one day. Alec knew that was possible.

The next days of so-called rest were spent washing and drying old uniforms in the vats that had been their baths, ready for the next group to be given leave. Then followed a boxing contest which didn't particularly interest Alec. In the evenings Jack produced his battered set of cards or sometimes songs were sung by all. Here We Go Again; Mademoiselle from Armentieres; I Want to Go Home; They Wouldn't Believe Me, and many others. After that it was time to march to the line and a rumour that a big battle was looming.

TEN

The Australian Third Division was back on the line to bury the dead. In the meantime the bombardment of the German lines continued at a furious pace, in preparation for future battles further north. Also in preparation for future battles, General Plummer ordered the Australians and New Zealanders to take German positions near what was known as the Warneton Line, in preparation for a feint towards Lille. Eleventh Brigade was tasked to establish a new trench system over ground taken during Messines, and that's where Martin became involved. Three new battalion headquarters were established in former German dugouts, and Martin was given a company of sappers to connect those dugouts to battle headquarters at the ruined shop at Armentieres.

They laid telephone cable north-east and closer to the new front line, and as they approached the new trench complex Martin was most impressed. A new advanced front line was dug; a series of bays, with fire-steps and traverses, was made immediately in advance of the old front line, which then became a traffic trench behind them. Six cross-trenches were made between the front and support lines. Given the size of their task Martin stayed on the line with his sappers, and over time the enemy took an interest in the proceedings on the opposite side of no man's land. Martin always found it difficult to sleep in trenches on muddy duckboards beneath a groundsheet, but the nightly noises from battles between patrols on both sides made sleep all but impossible. He heard it all: rifle fire, the odd trench mortar, flares bursting high with sharp 'cracks' before flooding the scene with bright, white light. The only thing that kept him going after sleepless nights was his morning cup of strong, black coffee.

Martin woke; strange that he had slept and maybe he was getting use to life on the line, and stared up at Corporal Dave Rice looking down on him.

"G'day Martin," Dave said with a big, toothy grin which exposed his missing molar.

Martin rubbed his eyes. "Hello Dave," he said wearily before glancing at his watch. Almost seven. He rubbed his eyes again. "Time for...."

"Coffee," and Dave brandished a steaming mug.

Martin sat up and used the sandbag wall as a backrest, and that coffee was a wonderful way to start the day.

"What's next?" Dave asked.

"Connection to forty-second's dugout and then we can test."

"We're nearly there."

They were a good crew and had done a great job so far. "Thanks Dave, and you and your men are so good you could have done this on your own."

Dave didn't look like he knew how to handle that compliment, and instead he left for his men who were ready to go, about a hundred yards short of the former German dugout now located off an Allied support trench. It was an amazing, spacious structure of brick, timber, steel and sandbags with electrical cabling for lights, no candles or kerosene lamps, and even partitioned latrines. Martin kept out of the way while they lifted the duckboards in the support trench, dug three foot deep trenches, laid the cable, re-laid the earth and replaced the duckboards. Steadily they worked their way to the dugout, and there Martin took over and connected the precious trench phone.

Suddenly all was chaos and mayhem as explosions rained down all about, and the enemy were at it again with trench mortars. Martin stayed where he was; unlike Allied dugouts it would take more than a shell or mortar to bring down that dugout. When it was over he went outside, and fortunately for his sappers the target had been the front line. There stretcher bearers were already tending the injured. In addition to regular nightly battles between patrols, there had been much trench mortar fire and some shelling to the rear.

"Martin...?" Tom asked apprehensively.

Martin faced the battalion signals officer; Second Lieutenant Tom White. "We're finished Tom," he said. "All we've got to do is test. I'll go to Armentieres and ring you, and if that works I'll hang up and you can ring me."

"Right-o Martin."

"Dave," Martin said. "Stay here with Tom until we test, and if that works you'll be free to go."

"Back to digging latrines," Dave said with a big, toothy smile.

Martin nodded thoughtfully and he hadn't thought about a sapper's life until then. But digging latrines, patching roads and laying duckboards was their lot for the war. With that thought in mind Martin took to the communication trench that headed towards the site of the former town of Messines, now reduced to rubble. Once out of rifle range Martin turned towards the south and crossed shell-ruined ground past silent artillery guns. Each gun battery had an above ground trench of sandbags, where the crew ate, slept and guarded. But all was quiet because General Monash planned to keep German interest out of that sector of the line as much as possible, until the time was right to advance to the Warneton Line. So the gunners waited at their silent batteries.

Until suddenly a shell burst about 30 yards away, and Martin had been there before. When a second shell exploded nearby, he ran towards the only cover which was the trench of the nearest battery. Only the next shell landed much closer and Martin felt a stinging, burning pain in his left shoulder. He broke stride before continuing and dived into the sandbagged enclosure and almost into the lap of a young gunner. He straightened himself and winced with the pain.

"You've been hit," the gunner said.

"I have," Martin replied, and his shoulder hurt really badly.

The shells kept raining down and Martin hoped their trench wasn't targeted. "I'll get the stretcher bearers," the young gunner with the grey eyes said.

"No don't; it's too dangerous."

"Bloody Huns," another gunner grumbled.

"My name's Alec," the young gunner said.

"I'm Martin."

"Pleased to meet you Martin."

"You too Alec."

"And here we have Frank, George, Bill, Jack and Bob."

"Pleased to meet you all."

"Do you know what's going on?" Alec asked.

154

Martin did of course, but he couldn't say. "I'm here to lay telephone cables to the new lines."

Alec nodded thoughtfully.

"Your turn will come when it's time," Martin said.

"We know this war can't be won without artillery," Alec said.

The shelling had stopped and Alec stood to look over their parapet. He wasn't tall, maybe five foot six, and in his early twenties. Martin pondered that. If it wasn't for his matriculation, Martin's war could have been with an artillery battery like those men, instead of commanding sappers and liaising with GSOs and even the General.

"How's your injury?" Alec asked.

"It hurts," Martin said truthfully.

"It's ruined your uniform."

Indeed it had, with a nasty tear and soaked with blood. But it was only his shoulder and he was mobile. "I'll be fine to walk with this. Do you know where the dressing station is?"

"I can take you."

"Thanks Alec."

Alec climbed out of the trench and put his hand down for Martin, who needed help given he was temporarily one-handed. And cradling his left arm to ease the pain, Martin walked across the pock-marked wasteland alongside Alec.

They walked in silence for some distance with Martin feeling strangely awkward at being rescued by an enlisted man.

"How long have you been here?" Martin eventually asked.

"A month," Alec said. "And you Martin?'

"Seven months. But we've both been away from home for a long time."

Alec nodded. "Yes, we have."

"The sooner this is over and we can return to where we belong; the better."

Ahead were white tents with camouflaged rooves surrounded by a bustle of activity. "Martin, this is it," Alec said.

"Thanks for bringing me here."

"That's no trouble."

Martin stopped and they shook hands. "Good luck with your war Alec."

"And you too Martin."

Martin watched the gunner turn towards his battery, and then he headed to the largest tent.

* * *

Martin was at the switchboard and in the background Major-General Monash looked on with his head tilted.

"Are you sure you should be here?" the General asked.

"Of course sir," Martin said. "My shoulder doesn't hurt and I'm much better here than wasting time in a hospital bed. My sling won't get in the way, I promise."

Monash nodded and early on a wet morning, three-fifty in the morning on the 31st of July, forty-second and forty-third battalions were ready to advance towards the windmill which defined the Warneton Line. As always the Major-General had planned the battle to some detail, leaving little to chance. And like Messines and the big raid, the battle of Windmill Ridge was a great success with all German posts taken within the designated half-hour. Troops dug-in and Martin's day was over by midday, although there were further casualties later in the day when German artillery, spotted by German observation aircraft, targeted the new Australian lines.

Preliminary casualties for the operation were more than 500 killed and injured, and as always Major-General Monash conducted an intensive debrief with those involved. Once that was complete the Third Australian Division was sent south for six weeks to rest, recruit, refit and re-train. Over the past months there were many deaths, injuries and of course sickness, including many in hospital having treatment for venereal disease contracted at the many brothels near the front. In fact, for every two to three soldiers wounded in action, one soldier was sent away for treatment of venereal disease. Martin felt partly embarrassed and partly smug that he too was a casualty, something he never expected, and relieved that he was able to discard his sling after about a month. Fortunately he fully recovered which was quite lucky, because the after-effects of shell shrapnel wounds could often be severe. Often very, very severe so he was a lucky man indeed.

ELEVEN

Third division left the ongoing bombardment behind and marched on foot towards Blequin; just inland from Boulogne-sur-Mer. It took four days marching with many songs on the way, before they reached the area. Martin, Harry and some of the officers of the division were billeted about a half-hour away in the pretty little town of Desvres. Martin and Harry had use of a bedroom in the neat little house belonging to Monsieur and Madame Duboit, and staying in a bedroom belonging to sons at war for France.

Desvres was untouched by war and almost untouched by time. It was a small village surrounded by lush, green forests, and based around several inner streets of shops with residences above. Away from the city centre were two-storey residences, including the pretty, stucco and brick home of the Duboit family on Rue de la Belle Croix. There was the inevitable village square surrounded by shops and the town hall, and further along was the largest building in the village: a church built in sturdy granite. As always in France there were women, children and old men, because most men of fighting age were away for the war effort.

After arriving around midday, Martin washed his uniform before bathing, and was ready later in the afternoon for a filling meal of mussels with vegetables and cheese. He was tired of having Harry trailing him, especially after their time in Paris, and he wanted to explore on his own. He told Harry he was going out which really meant out alone, and Martin headed towards Place de Léon Blum. It was a long, rectangular square lined by neat two and three-storey buildings in stone or stucco, some with attic windows built into high-pitched slate rooves. There were several officers taking in the sights, and one restaurant and cafe on the far side of the square; a modest two-storey building maybe 100 years old or so. Martin strolled to the Restaurant Café Central and went inside the smoky room, quiet but for hushed conversations from several officers of various ranks, but mostly lieutenants like himself. Dark green walls, dark green leather-covered chairs and dark-stained timberwork made it a sombre place; especially with lights dulled by heavy, crystal shades. Martin went to the bar where an older gentleman, as all men working in France were older, waited.

"Bonsoir Monsieur," Martin said. "Je voudrais un whisky et un cigar si'l vous plais."

"Deux francs Monsieur,"

Martin opened his wallet and placed two notes on the counter. The barman grabbed a bottle of Aberlour single malt and poured a small tumbler, and then placed a polished, timber box on the counter for Martin to select his cigar. Martin held one for the barman to cut the end, and then the barman lit a long match and Martin played the end of the cigar over the flame. Once lit he breathed the cigar normally while savouring the smoky scent. He turned around and surveyed the room, cigar in one hand and drink in the other, but nobody at the dozen or more tables interested him. In fact it was deadly dull and needed brightening. Martin wondered about the piano against the far wall. He went to it, grabbing an ashtray from a table on the way, and sat at the stool. He put his drink on top and played a simple C-major scale, and surprisingly the piano seemed in tune. He ran his finger from end to end and it truly was in tune. Martin knew it by heart, he practiced it enough, and even if it wasn't good enough to pass his exam, he knew it was good enough. Chopin is cannons buried in flowers, not cannons buried in cannons she said, but in the midst of war cannons buried in cannons were appropriate. What would have made Martin more comfortable was a score rather than relying on his memory. He stood and checked under the seat, and amidst some Schubert sonatas and popular songs were the opus 58 sonata and also the sixth polonaise. Martin rested his cigar on the ashtray, arranged the scores and got comfortable, and hit the opening chord hard just like that failed exam. Hard most of the way through the opening allegro maestoso, hard indeed. Certainly hard enough to pause conversations for several minutes.

Part-way through a woman came to the piano and stood side-on, watching him. Martin almost lost his way before regaining his composure, and continued to the end of that movement. He turned his head to acknowledge her.

"Vous êtes magnifique Monsieur!" she exclaimed.

Martin smoked his cigar while he studied her: petite, fair - very fair. In her twenties; maybe mid-twenties or maybe older. She wore a lovely outfit: a white and purple patterned blouse, a long, purple satin skirt, and a ring on the third finger of her left hand. "Merci Madame," Martin said.

"Encore en fois?" she asked, again.

"There's more," Martin said in French.

Martin butted his cigar, turned the page and she looked over his shoulder. "You can read that?" she asked, frowning.

"It's not hard," Martin said. "It's like reading another language. I'll play the next movement."

She nodded and Martin played the slower and less dramatic scherzo. It was a much shorter movement, followed by a long and delicate largo. Then he paused and looked up at his audience. "Je m'apelle Lieutenant Martin Ward," he said. "Australien."

"Ah oui. Je m'apalle Madame Belaire."

"There's one more part."

Madame Belaire looked sad for a split second until Martin played the dramatic opening chord of the presto, which was his favourite movement with an unusual galloping, almost syncopated rhythm. It was quite short, and Martin liked it so much that he wished it was longer. At the end he took his glass and sipped some whisky.

"How can you play like that, Lieutenant Ward?" Madame Belaire asked.

"I practiced it many times for an exam," Martin said.

"Do you know anything else?"

"I have music for one more." Martin looked deeply into her lovely, brown eyes. "Just for you."

She didn't take her gaze off him and didn't flinch.

Martin put his glass down and browsed the score for the polonaise because he didn't know it well, even though he had played it several times in the past. He nodded while it came back and then he commenced. It was a difficult piece but Martin muddled through it well enough, although he was glad when it was over.

"I don't know how you can play that," Madame Belaire said.

Martin moved to the left of the bench. "Sit beside me and I'll show you."

She sat close, her leg brushing his leg, and Martin pointed at the first note of the first chord. "This one is this one," he said, taking her hand and placing her finger on the note. "And this one is this one." Martin took her fingers and played the chord. And then he took her long, slim fingers while thinking that women might have a natural advantage with the piano. He pointed out the next two notes and guided her to strike them, and the next two and the next two until she played the right hand part of the opening two bars.

"That's how you read music and play the piano," he said.

"Merci," she said. "Perhaps I will learn to play the piano one day."

"Playing the piano is a way of bringing normality to lives which have been disconnected."

"You have come a long way to liberate my country."

"Many have come a long way to liberate your country."

"What do you think of the traitorous mutineers?"

Martin was shocked because that was only a rumour and was supposed to be a secret. He wondered what to say without lying, and then it came to him. "I have come to France to do my duty as best I can," Martin said. "I hope I can make a difference."

"I understand. You're resting here?"

"We're resting until some exercises in about two weeks. Then we will return to the line to continue the fight."

"Will we win?"

"We will win."

"Where are you staying?"

"I'm sharing a room in town." Madame Belaire was so close that he felt her leg against his, and she sat close like that for a reason. She was interested in him. "Where are you staying Madame Belaire?" Martin asked.

"I have a room upstairs. This cafe belongs to a traitorous mutineer."

Martin nodded while he digested that comment. She was beautiful, most certainly alone, and interested in him. He gazed into her lovely, brown eyes again. "You can call me Martin," he said.

"You can call me Simone."

"Simone, is your room comfortable?"

"It is."

Martin stood and took her hand, and she rose and they went along a corridor to a narrow staircase. Simone climbed creaking stairs until she reached a corridor at the top, dark green and with lights heavily shaded. She opened the first door and went into a modest bed chamber, again in dark green and lit by a shaded bedside light. A bed nested beneath a soft, white quilt between black, iron bedheads, with dark mahogany bedside tables on either side; a dark mahogany wardrobe to one side, a dark mahogany dressing table opposite and a washbasin next to that. Martin closed the door behind him and took Simone in his arms, and delighted in the soft curves of her femininity. They kissed lip to lip and then tongue to tongue before Simone broke it off. She reached behind and unbuttoned her blouse while Martin removed his tunic, her skirt and his boots, her chemise and his shirt, her corset and his breeches, her petticoat and his vest, her drawers and his underwear, and then she was naked but for black stockings. She sat on the bed and removed them carefully, and then stood and Martin hugged her once more, resting his hands on her firm, fleshy buttocks, her small, firm breasts pressing against his chest. He kissed her lip to lip and tongue to tongue for an age, before breaking it off and turning the sheet and the feather quilt back. Simone climbed on and Martin admired her fair beauty before joining her to kiss again. He traced kisses lower and lower and lower and she started. He looked up and their eyes met, and he nodded hoping to reassure her. He traced his tongue lightly at first and then more and then much more. He looked up at her pretty face before rolling onto his back.

Simone moved and Martin held her soft buttocks while she made love to him eye to eye, her eyes sparkling in the muted light. Closer and closer, he saw her and felt her, and then he nudged her and took her hard. He collapsed with his head on her breasts and she ran her fingers through his damp hair.

"You could stay the night but you have no nightgown," Simone eventually said.

Martin lifted his head and looked into her eyes. "We should sleep together like this."

"Yes, we should."

Martin switched off the light and dragged the soft, feather quilt to cover them both, and still intertwined they fell asleep.

* * *

Martin woke to find Simone, still naked, looking at him with her head propped on her hand.

"Bonjour mon cheri," she said.

"Bonjour ma cherié," he replied.

She swallowed as if something was on her mind.

"Do you want to make love?" Martin asked in French.

She nodded her head while biting her lip.

Martin rolled onto his back and she made love to him like the evening before. And like the evening before Martin took her which was the best way, because after he could lie body to body and kiss her beautiful soft lips while she played with his hair.

"What work do you do in Australia?" Simone asked.

"I was a sailor," Martin said. "I lived in a place called New Guinea which is north of Australia, and I took a Red Cross doctor and nurse to islands and settlements."

"You don't seem like a sailor."

"That came to me by chance, and then I realised that while sailing wouldn't make me a wealthy man, there are greater riches to be had than mere money."

"You're an interesting man."

Martin knew he had an unusual past. "I'm billeted in Desvres for the next five weeks. I can bring my things here."

"Including your nightgown?"

"I won't need a nightgown."

"You won't. We should wash and dress and I can make you breakfast."

Love-making followed by breakfast with coffee sounded like the most magnificent way to start the day. And then Martin felt a momentary ache of longing for the lovely woman he left behind. Many times they made love followed by breakfast with coffee. He wondered how she was.

"What is it mon cheri?" Simone asked.

Martin wondered what it really was. "Love and happiness despite insanity all around," he said.

"It'll be over one day."

Martin really hoped so.

* * *

Martin climbed the stairs of the little house on Rue de la Belle Croix to his room, where Harry sat on the bed while writing a letter.

"Good morning Harry," Martin said.

"G'day Martin," Harry said. "You're looking cheerful this morning."

"I've come to get my things. From now on you can have this room to yourself."

"I heard something happened. Something to do with a piano?"

"I met someone."

"She's married."

"She's lonely."

"But still...."

"She's lonely."

"What's her name?"

"Simone."

"That's a nice name."

"She's a nice woman. Are you writing to Edith?"

"Yes."

Martin sat on the other bed. "As you know I don't have a sweetheart," he said.

"I know, and now you have Simone."

"Until we leave I have Simone. If anyone needs me I'll be at Restaurant Café Central on Place de Léon Blum."

Martin packed his meagre belongings into his kit and slung it over his shoulder. With a farewell to cheerful Harry he returned to the cafe and climbed the stairs to Simone's room to leave his bag. She wasn't there so he went to the spacious kitchen: a stainless steel bench with sink beneath the window, and racks above holding pots, pans and all manner of utensils. On the far wall were two ranges, one coal and one gas, and opposite were two ice chests and a large cupboard with two louvered doors. In the centre was a well-worn square table and four, worn chairs. Simone had a cane hamper on that table and she looked up.

"Would you like a picnic lunch?" she asked.

"Yes, that would be delightful," Martin said.

"Unfortunately with the shortages...."

Martin knew.

Simone sliced rolls of bread lengthwise, and stuffed that with ham, some boiled eggs and some lettuce. Then followed a bottle of white wine still dripping with condensation, and two glasses. "We are prepared," she said proudly.

Martin took the hamper and they headed outside where officers of third division were taking in the sights of the little village. Martin ignored them but eyes followed the couple, Simone wearing a simple white blouse, a black skirt and a black beret pinned at an angle. She was beautiful and probably close in age to Martin. The bitterness of war had made her seem older than her years. She led the way out of the little town and towards a forest, and then along a path which ended at a lake surrounded by trees and shrubs, still thick and green in early autumn. It was lovely and peaceful with the only sign of life being several ducks bobbing in the water.

"Le Mont Pelé," Simone said before sitting on the grassy bank.

"It's beautiful," Martin said before sitting to join her. He imagined some years before, a young man and a young woman picnicking at that spot, until war came and took him away.

"While you were away I looked up an encyclopaedia on New Guinea."

Martin imagined what she read. "Those articles are superficial," he said. "In New Guinea I travelled to coastal villages where the men go fishing and the women do basic farming of yams, and gathering of breadfruit, bananas and other foods. They live comfortably; in peace and harmony with their surroundings."

"There were pictures."

"They dress simply, and it's hot and often humid there. They don't see a woman's breasts as taboo." Martin wondered what more to say. "The people of New Guinea are capable, and always friendly and cheerful. It's a peaceful, tropical paradise, and more beautiful than you could ever imagine."

Simone nodded thoughtfully before gazing towards the still waters of the lake. "We should eat," she eventually said.

Simone removed the wine, took a corkscrew and extracted the cork, and poured two glasses. Martin inhaled the lovely, oak scent before sipping some. Simone gave him a roll on a plate, which was wonderful, fresh and crusty.

"I would give anything to see the world and live in New Guinea," Simone said.

Martin nodded in agreement, while deciding not to tell Simone that life for European women wasn't the same. He finished his roll and sipped more of his wine, and momentarily he thought of Jara. But that was long past and now he was with Simone. He turned his head and with her fine features, her hazel eyes and chestnut-brown hair, she was so French. "I'm glad to be here with you," Martin said, and he really meant that.

"I'm glad to be here with you too." She grabbed his face. "My heart has been broken and I feel lonely," she said. "Make me feel better."

"I felt lonely, but not anymore."

She held his face and gazed deep into his eyes for so long, before turning away to take her glass. She finished her wine and pondered her empty glass. "Market is on today," she said. "I need to buy for the cafe. Do you want to help me?"

"Of course," Martin said.

Simone stood and reached down for his hand. "Let's take this basket back and then I will show you the sights of our little village."

Martin placed the cork in the half-empty bottle, gathered the plates and glasses and fastened the hamper, and he stood to be shown the sights of Desvres. The market was trestle tables set up in Place de Léon Blum, with local farmers and their wives selling local produce. Chicken, eggs, cuts of meat, late season fruit. Simone was pleased with what she bought, which was mostly packed into the ice chests in the kitchen. Martin was introduced to the cook Charlotte and the waitress Alice, and he was told that Monsieur Albert worked evenings behind the bar. Martin was invited to keep the women company while they prepared for the evening meal; bound to be busy with the Australians in town he was told. Ensconced at the table in the kitchen it felt dreamlike to listen to Simone and Charlotte talking, gossiping, in another language in a cafe far from his home. The two women were close friends more than employer and employee, and Martin liked that.

Later when the Australian officers appeared for meals, Martin went to the bar and bought a whisky but not a cigar, and went to the piano stool and found a strange mixture of popular songs, Schubert and more Chopin. He passed the time playing Schubert quietly while Alice and Monsieur Albert both had busy nights. The last diners left around ten and Martin went to the kitchen where Simone and Charlotte washed plates. Martin took a seat at the table and waited for them to finish, and the last of the three employees of the little cafe bid 'bon nuit' before Simone locked the door and turned off the lights downstairs. Sleep came easily in the modest bedchamber near the top of the stairs.

* * *

They made love the following morning, and after they had coffee and bread in the kitchen. Martin wanted to know so much, in a way despite the intimacy they shared they were strangers, but he knew that Simone would tell him when the time was right for her. She played with her empty mug.

"We open Mondays to Saturdays at midday for lunch, and stay open until nine or when the last leave," she said while still playing with her mug. "Sunday is our break."

"It's busy with the officers in town."

She nodded. "Yes it is. At other times it's not so busy but we get by well enough."

"I like this cafe."

Simone nodded. "I do too," she eventually said. "This is home and work together and I once liked that, but...," and she shrugged her shoulders.

Upstairs had a sitting room, two bedrooms and a bathroom. Martin opened the curtains and explored the sitting room which had a couch and two chairs covered in cream and floral cloth, a fireplace with a clock on the mantel, a table and a bookcase which contained volumes of encyclopaedias and French women's romance novels, which clearly belonged to Simone. She came into the room carrying a newspaper and sat in the other chair.

"I have some cards in my kit," Martin said.

"I don't like cards," Simone said.

She liked reading the newspaper and reading cheap novels. Martin got his cards, brought the table around and laid out a game of solitaire. She sensed Simone watching him and looked into her lovely, hazel eyes.

"You must do that a lot," she said.

"I share a hut and sometimes we play cards together, and sometimes I play this."

"Did you play cards in New Guinea?"

Martin nodded. "Yes a lot." He remembered long nights beneath clear, starry nights like they were yesterday. Simone went back to her reading and Martin went back to his cards, and he guessed that was the way the day would play out, until towards midday when it was time to get the cafe ready for lunch.

* * *

Martin climbed the stairs of Chateau d'Hervarre two at a time and burst into the entry hall. He strode with the noise from his boots echoing all around. To his right the former parlour was hushed busyness with the senior officers discussing plans for forthcoming training exercises. Many thousands of recruits had been sent to third division after training in England, and they had to be trained the Major-General Monash way and prepared for life on the front lines. One face looked up and broke into a smile, Major Wieck, the latest General Staff Officer. "Lieutenant Ward," he said. "You're looking cheerful. The rest has done you good."

"It has indeed sir," Martin said, while glancing at Harry smiling brightly in the background.

"We will be undertaking exercises over the next few weeks, so your expertise in keeping our communications lines open will be invaluable."

"I will do my best sir."

"Especially being so cheerful."

"That too sir."

Major Wieck left the room and went upstairs. Harry came to Martin. "How's life with Simone," he asked.

"Life with Simone is quite fine if you speak French, because she doesn't speak a word of English."

"Is that right?"

Martin nodded. "It is. But never you mind because you have Edith. How is she?"

"Getting over a cold in her last letter, but otherwise fine. Too far away though."

"This war won't last forever and you can imagine how it will be when you're together again."

"Sometimes I do," Harry said very, very quietly. "What plans do you have?" he asked.

Martin pondered. "We're billeted at Deserves for the next four weeks," he said. "After that I don't know."

Harry's face darkened.

"Simone's married," Martin said. "I feel that her marriage has come to an end for various reasons, but I can't make plans."

Harry still didn't look convinced.

"She said her husband was involved in the mutiny," Martin said.

"How does she know?" Harry asked, looking surprised

"I don't know, but perhaps word got through to her."

"Well if her husband mutinied then that explains a lot."

Martin wasn't sure. "If positions were reversed and you refused to fight, perhaps after being pushed too hard with insufficient rest and recovery, how would Edith react?"

"She would forgive me."

"That's right. I'm no expert on love, but if you love someone then you forgive them for a mistake."

"Do you love Simone?"

Martin wondered what love was, and if love was where your one and only soulmate was your reason for existence, then that wasn't what he had with Simone. "I like Simone and she likes me, and that's what we have for the next few weeks." Martin tried to make sense of their relationship from Simone's perspective, and perhaps she needed the company of a man who she liked rather than loved. "War's a strange thing," he eventually said.

Major Wieck came down the stairs. "Lieutenant Ward," he said. "You might as well go to the training. Head along Route des Calais towards Desvres, and part-way along there's an intersection with Rue du Val and an unnamed road which heads north. We're training in there."

"Yes sir."

Martin walked out of the old chateau and turned around to admire the strange building. It was a massive, white building with a large, round tower at one end, topped with a tall, pointed roof. Martin would have sworn that tower was part of an older castle from medieval times, and the remainder of the chateau was built against it. He shrugged his shoulders before walking along a path lined by tall trees, and then turned onto Rue de l'Eglise and headed north. He walked past beautiful, rolling hills covered by lush, green pastures with stands of shady trees dotted here and there. After about 20 minutes he heard rather than saw the training; thousands of voices carried across the delightful, French countryside. Martin crested a hill and closed on the reserve set aside for training, which was a large, grassy area with forest further along. On the left infantrymen dug trenches, while on the right there was a cricket match underway. Cricket was more interesting than trenches so

Martin went to the crowd gathered around, and there was a crowd within a crowd so Martin went there.

"Who's playing?" Martin asked one of the enlisted men who was centre of attention.

"Infantry versus artillery," was the reply. "Want to bet?"

"Who do you reckon?"

"Infantry of course."

"Give me two bob on the gunners."

Two coins were exchanged for a slip and Martin left the bookmaker to check up on the progress of the game. Artillery was batting and was one for thirty-eight, which was a solid start.

"G' day Martin!"

Martin spun around to spot Alf closing. "Hello Alf," he said.

"How's things with your...?"

"Fine thanks. It's been a while since we talked."

"It has; Messines worked well."

"Too many casualties though."

"I know mate and I've got an idea on that. I spoke to some of the blokes who went over, and they reckon we ought to do away with the weeks of bombardment before the battle and do it on the day instead."

"You're joking!" Martin exclaimed.

Alf shook his head. "They were serious. The bombardment's supposed to clear the barbed wire and flatten the breastworks, but whatever damage we do to the wire's repaired by the Hun. They seem 'em and hear 'em every night; even the night before battle. But the thing is when the guns start it's like putting up a dirty great sign that we're coming for 'em. So they dig deep, bring up their reserves out of range, and they're ready and waiting."

Martin thought about what Alf said, and if the barbed wire was repaired right up to the night of battle, there was no need to shell except.... "We should time the bombardment for when the men go over, aiming at the wire and breastworks and creeping backwards from there. And counter-barrage their guns at the same time."

"That's right mate."

The cricket match wasn't that interesting but Alf's observation was. He ought to head back to the chateau and tell Major Wieck. No it was Alf's observation and Alf should tell Major Wieck. "Do you want to go for a walk mate?" Martin asked.

"Why not?"

They headed away and Martin asked about how the battle communications worked for Alf's battalion, and it worked almost too well if such thing were possible. He was almost inundated with progress reports coming from runners and from HQ. Just as they rounded a curve in the road Martin spotted the major heading towards the training ground. Martin stopped near a stand of trees and waited.

"We meet again," Major Wieck said.

"You can't help bad luck sir," Martin replied. "Major Wieck, this is Second Lieutenant Alf Sanderson, signals officer of thirty-seven battalion, and he's got an interesting idea for us."

"Well then Lieutenant Sanderson; let's hear what you've got."

"I told Martin what I found out from the blokes from the trenches, and they reckon we shouldn't shell the Hun until the battle starts. Whatever damage we're doing to their barbed wire's repaired night by night, and because we're shelling 'em they know we're coming and they're ready for us. They dig deep and keep their reserves just out of range."

Major Wieck nodded slowly. "So if we don't shell until the moment of battle, we catch them unprepared?"

"We would. Our first barrage should be on their wire and breastworks, and then creeping backwards from there, and of course counter-barrage their guns with gas."

"That's risky if it doesn't work."

"But if it works; can you imagine the chaos?" Martin said. He thought about their situation. "The plebiscite's been defeated so we've got what we've got; and if we want to win this war we've got to do it smarter and not harder. Messines was smart in many ways, and this idea takes that concept one stage further."

"You're right," Major Wieck said. He then broke into a big smile. "Imagine a Pommy infantryman telling a Pommy lieutenant how to win the war, and then a Pommy lieutenant telling a Pommy major?"

"It's just as well that we're Aussies."

"That's for sure. Do you know what's going on with the training?"

"I've got two bob on artillery to beat infantry at cricket, sir."

"Well we'd better see how the game's going. That could make you a wealthy man."

"I always knew I'd find the reason why I enlisted."

TWELVE

The men of forty-seventh battery pounded the enemy, along
with the artillery of other Australian batteries, the British and
the New Zealanders. From early until late, they fired shells
at an unseen and unknown enemy while knowing they were
doing the right thing. In August, the weather changed to
cold with rain for two weeks, and the battlefield turned into a
dreadful, muddy mess. There wasn't any way for the men of
the battery to get away from the mud. Even when resting on
the boards in their above-ground trench of sandbags, mud
oozed everywhere. The rain at night was particularly bad,
with the only shelter being to sleep under groundsheets.
They took turns at guard duty, and being on guard all night
in the rain was particularly trying. The only respite was relief
to an abandoned school at Steenwerck, where in rooms
devoid of furniture but for hessian sacks to sleep on and a
blackboard on a wall; they had a roof over their head for a
week. Alec tried not to think of mattresses, sheets and
blankets; for soldiers those things didn't exist. It was boards
and mud or a cold room and hessian. At Steenwerck they
were put to unloading trains at sidings near the station;
artillery shells mostly but other supplies as well. At least
while on relief Alec got to wash outside beneath a perforated

tin of cold water with a tap, clean his uniform, and especially clean away as much lice as possible. They played cards, wrote letters, smoked cigarettes for those who smoked, and got to know the gunners from other batteries before returning to the line. By then the rain had passed and the ground slowly dried. There they bombarded the enemy, the range called by Paul Allen for the six batteries under his care, and always under the threat of enemy shells. Other batteries were hit; fellow gunners killed and maimed, but the worst was when a shell landed just behind and took poor Paul's head off. That shell was so close, too close, and Alec turned around at the wrong moment to see what happened. He threw up while the other members of the battery stood with mouths hanging open, and they still stood silent while the stretcher bearers gathered up what was left of the poor corporal and carried him away. Alec didn't know Paul well but he was older, perhaps in his thirties and probably married, which meant another widow in Australia.

David Else took over for the rest of the day, and the next day they had Corporal Ted Pratt. Ted was a man of few words, taciturn, and Alec guessed that he'd seen a lot.

At the end of the week the men of forty-seventh battery were relieved to the school at Steenwerck, and they settled into a routine of alternating week in and week out.

The twentieth of September saw an early start; up at dawn to commence a creeping bombardment at five-forty, with the range changes called by Ted Pratt as usual. While that was going on, engineers commenced to build roads across a wasteland strewn with shell craters, and that attracted more than the usual attention of enemy artillery. Alec didn't know what the next part of the bigger plan was, but he knew it involved his battery and his brigade. The new roads led from their current position towards an area known as Polygon Wood, but that wood was just a miserable patch of dead trees and churned-over ground. In time those roads would be used to move their guns, and to bring ammunition after that move. There was a lot of enemy interest towards the road building with many more shells coming over than normal, some quite close and spraying dirt and debris near the men at the gun. Towards evening after a long day, they were stood down for their usual meal of tinned stew and a cup of tea. Alec sat with his back to their stack of shells and poked at his stew to see if could actually find some meat in the watery mess.

"I could do without this bloody road going through," Jack grumbled. "Too many Hun shells for my liking."

"How do you reckon they know what's going on?" George asked.

"They've got the high ground on Passchendaele Ridge," Bob said. "From there they can see everything we do."

"Is that right?"

"It is."

Alec sipped his tea. "I could do without this road," he said. "We've been lucky since Paul got it, but today stretched that luck."

"You're right," Frank said.

Alec shrugged his shoulders. "There's nothing we can do about it."

"If you're a believer then pray," George said optimistically.

Alec thought that was all they could do. He finished the last of his stew and drank the last of his tea before yawning and stretching. "I'm all worn-out," he said.

"Early night?" George asked.

Alec yawned again. "Yes, an early night."

Alec went to their trench to unfurl his greatcoat to make up his bed on the dry, dirt of Flanders, and he lay on his coat with his helmet by his side. In the background were the never-ending sounds of the front line: booms of artillery, the odd rifle shot, men's shouts; the crack of flares bursting high. On his back, Alec drifted off to sleep.

* * *

Alec woke with a start. He looked up into the sun to see Ted Pratt looking down at him. Alec stretched and sat up, and saw his colleagues were sleeping soundly except Bob on guard duty.

"Our blokes are in trouble," Ted said.

Alec nodded. "I'll get something to eat." He got up, rolled up his coat and put it by his kit, put on his helmet, grabbed his mug and headed to the mess tents about ten minutes walk away. While he queued for tea and some biscuits, the men from forty-seventh battery fell into line. Alec was served, helped himself to some condensed milk and sugar for his drink, and he walked to the battery while soaking a biscuit to make it soft enough to eat. Suddenly he heard that dreadful, dull whistle and instinctively ducked. The shell hit about 80 yards away with a huge explosion and dirt was thrown all over. Immediately followed another and another and then silence; all over for the moment. Alec continued his walk, minus half his tea which he ended up spilling. But that was a small price to pay.

"You alright Alec?" Jack called out.

Alec turned around. "I'm alright." He sighed. "Don't worry Jack; when a shell's got your name on it, it will get you then and not before."

"Yeah mate, I know."

Alec returned to their trench, stowed his mug, went to the gun and got ready to adjust the range. Ted told Alec to aim for 2,200 yards, and with Jack on the trigger they started work; shell after shell after shell. When the time seemed right they changed with Jack on range and Alec unloading the casings. The next change saw Alec on the stockpile of shells handing them to George, one after the other. By that time the mist was lifting and it was getting quite warm. Alec was about to take off his tunic when he heard that dreaded, dull whistling; closer and closer and closer; too close. He threw himself on the ground for protection just as a terrible explosion seemingly rocked the ground and sprayed dirt over everything. Pressed hard against the ground he looked to one side when another one came in, and he wished for their sandbagged trench. It wasn't much protection but it was something. Alec was about to get up when he heard the next one, and the explosion was followed by a ripping, burning pain in his leg. He lay there waiting for the next shell but nothing happened. Indeed it was eerily silent.

"Alec...?" Jack asked.

"I've been hit on my leg," Alec said.

"Shit!" Silence. "Get the stretcher bearers!"

Alec rolled onto his back and the pain from his left leg was terribly bad. Terribly, terribly bad. Over there, just yards away, George was gone. Dismembered. Alec looked away.

"Where're the fucking stretcher bearers?" Jack shouted.

"It's alright," Alec said even though the pain in his leg was terrible. At least he was alive.

"This is going to hurt mate," the voice said, and Alec looked up to the stranger who wore a white armband with a red cross. "We'll have you on your way in no time," he said, putting his hands under Alec's arms. Someone grabbed Alec's legs and he grunted with the tearing pain. The picked him up and moments later the pain subsided to a deadly, dull ache. "Do you need morphine?"

Anything but morphine. "No; I'm fine," Alec said.

They hoisted the stretcher and Alec looked to the side while he was carried away. Everything was as if nothing had happened. Totally normal, or as normal as a battlefield was going to be. On and on he was carried, past the rear lines and lounging soldiers smoking while they rested. On and on until Alec saw a farm surrounded by activity, with many stretcher bearers approaching with many casualties, and many green ambulances with big white circles and red crosses waiting. Alec was taken inside a low-roofed brick barn: cleaned out and fitted with benches along the sides and along the centre between timber roof supports, but still with the original dirt floor. Alec was helped from his stretcher and he had to wait amongst the casualties: mostly infantry with muddy uniforms, torn in some cases, soaked in blood in some cases, bandaged in some cases, very badly hurt in some cases, and many silently smoking while they waited. The worst was the man who'd lost half his face. Alec glanced at him, his jaw and teeth clearly visible, and then turned away to give that man privacy. Four medics in uniform worked hard dealing with the influx of patients from the battle. Alec waited with his painful leg stretched out while one of the medics treated a sergeant next to him. The sergeant had a long gash on his left arm, and the medic cleaned away the dried blood, treated the cut with antiseptic and applied a bandage before the sergeant was allowed to leave. The medic came to Alec.

"G'day mate," he said. "I'm Peter."

"Hello Peter; I'm Alec."

Peter squatted. "Let's see what we can do for you." He frowned. "I'll bind your wound to stop the blood and then we'll send you to the CCS."

Alec nodded while Peter cut his trouser leg with a pair of scissors. The antiseptic stung harshly, and the bandaging hurt and it took quite a while.

Peter stood. "Can you walk?" he asked.

Alec doubted it. "Not without help."

"Alright; I'll help you outside."

Peter bent down and Alec grabbed him with his right arm. Hobbling on his good, leg didn't hurt at all, and they went to the ambulances parked outside. There a driver leaned against his ambulance while smoking.

"Patient for the CCS," Peter said, and the driver took Alec and helped him into the back to lie alongside an infantryman bandaged around the waist and moaning lightly. Soon they were on their way, and after about 10 minutes Alec noticed large tents with camouflaged rooves. Large tents with rows of shapes to one side, and as they closed he saw what those shapes were. Dead bodies in uniform left outside to be buried, and worse was the large pit dug beyond; a mass grave. Alec shuddered. The driver stopped roughly with squealing brakes, and two stretcher bearers came to the rear of the ambulance where they lifted the stretcher containing the infantryman with the blood-soaked bandage. Alec waited for his turn, and soon after the stretcher bearers took him through a flap tied open and into a similar, hushed silence as the dressing station. There were rows of camp beds and many men with torn uniforms stained red. He saw four nurses in uniforms of white and grey, and a doctor in a white coat splattered with blood.

"Left leg," one of the nurses said flatly. "Over there."

They placed Alec's stretcher onto the wooden floor of the tent. It really hurt when they lifted him onto the bed, and then Alec was on his back on a canvas bed.

"Hello there soldier," a nurse with a clipboard said. "What's your name?"

"Alexander Morey, Alec."

"Rank, number and unit?"

"Gunner, 27606, twelfth field artillery battalion."

"Don't you worry Alec; we'll look after you as soon as we can."

"Thank you nurse."

Alec waited in the midst dull groans of pain, and although his leg hurt he wasn't as bad as some of the men there. The doctor dealt with the infantryman just arrived, and Alec knew that poor man was in a bad way. Alec looked away and then he sensed someone nearby and looked up at the doctor.

"Hello Alec; I'm Dr Louis Middleton and we'll see what we can do for you." The doctor touched Alec's leg and then unwound the bandage. Alec watched him peel the material back while frowning. He looked at Alec. "I'm sorry but we'll have to amputate."

Alec's heart jumped. "Amputate!" he exclaimed. "Is there any other way?"

"I'm afraid not; your bone's been broken in many places and there's a lot of shrapnel."

"I'm a cricketer...."

"I'm sorry but with shrapnel you'll get infected by dirt from the explosion. You wait here and we'll come for you when we're ready."

Alec lay alone on his bed. *Surely they didn't have to cut his leg off; surely there was a better way?* He never expected to get hurt let alone loose his leg. He was going to be cut-up and destroyed and not be a man anymore. *Bloody war; he never should have enlisted; white feathers or not!* Alec watched the doctor bending over another bed and telling another soldier more devastating news. Alec waited, cursing the war, until the nurse came to him.

"I have to inject you now," she said, before unbuttoning Alec's tunic to expose his arm. The injection didn't hurt compared to the dull pain of his leg, and a few moments later Alec felt strangely blissful and peaceful. Two uniformed stretcher bearers came to his bed.

"G'day mate; it's time for your operation."

Alec was lifted onto a tall, wheeled stretcher, had a blanket draped over and taken to another tent smelling of chloroform. The operating tent. There a doctor in a white coat splattered with blood waited beside a stainless steel table. A second doctor was at the end, and a nurse was opposite with a stainless steel trolley full of instruments. Alec was lifted onto the stainless steel table and the doctor at the end placed a gauze mask over Alec's face. The mask was sickly sweet and Alec felt very, very tired. Despite all that was happening to him he drifted away.

* * *

Alec woke and he didn't know where he was, except that his leg hurt badly. His leg hurt really, really badly. He had trouble opening his eyes; it was strange not to be able to open his eyes, but by concentrating he did and saw he was in a large tent filled with beds. The casualty clearing station somewhere behind the lines. His eyes flickered close and then open.

"How are you Alec?"

Alec looked at the hazy figure of a nurse. "My leg hurts a lot."

"That's normal but your operation went well. We'll send you to the hospital in Calais."

Alec felt so very tired. He drifted away but woke when he was being picked up from his bed and placed him on a wheeled stretcher. He was rolled outside, and there he was put into the lower part of a two-level stretcher cart on rails, and Alec felt like a piece of freight. A worthless piece of freight; used up and discarded. They placed another man on top, and the two casualties were wheeled away in the cart which ran on tramlines. Alec knew where they were going; he saw it when he arrived less than four months before. The station at Steenwerck, and his life had come a full circle.

THIRTEEN

Alec lifted the sheet and looked to make sure. He felt his leg and it was there, but it wasn't. Amputated about half-way between his knee and his ankle, and the lower part of what remained was wrapped in a bandage. It hurt. It hurt a lot. *Bloody war! Bloody, bloody war!*

"Hello Alec," Nurse Davis said. "How are you this morning?"

"It's very painful," Alec said. "Sometimes it feels like all of my leg's still there."

"That's normal. Do you need morphine for your pain?"

Morphine was a terrible drug. "No; I think I can manage," Alec said

A doctor came to his bed. "Well Gunner Morey; you're ready for travel and soon we'll have you away from here. It takes some time after an amputation before you can be fitted for an artificial leg. Your stump will shrink over time and we have to wait."

Having his leg being referred to as a stump sent a shiver up Alec's spine. "What happens next?" Alec asked.

"Hospital in England for a few months. There's also the possibility of gangrene from a shell injury such as yours."

"Why is that?"

"An exploding shell contains dirt and other material which can re-infect your wound."

Alec nodded and thought about the hundreds of shells he sent across the line to maim and kill German soldiers. For sure Germany started the war, but it wasn't fair on ordinary German soldiers to suffer like he did. And he inflicted that suffering on hundreds or more. "War is evil," Alec said quietly.

"No truer words ever spoken. Good luck Gunner Morey."

The doctor went to the next patient who was in a worse state: a double amputation. Alec picked up the book given to him by Nurse Davis and opened it at his bookmark. Lord Tony's Wife was good and not what Alec expected.

After a few days at the General Hospital at Calais, strangely converted from a hotel in the city centre, Alec was placed on a stretcher for his next journey. So far so good, and if he'd lost part of his left leg then so be it. He survived and many didn't, and he knew he could manage life as he was, as long as he could manage pain that never went away. In one of the many ambulances waiting in the street, they put Alec alongside three others for a short drive to the docks. There he was carried onto a hospital ship marked with large, red crosses. On the ship he was assigned one of eight bunks in a cabin. The bunks were taken by Pommy mates to share the journey. Alec couldn't understand why they were so accepting of their injuries. Surely they cursed the war and cursed what happened? Nurses called into the cabin every few hours to check on their patients, but all was as well as could be expected. After a time they were fed and that took away Alec's hunger and thirst. But that didn't help how he felt: a useless cripple in a room full of cripples/.

Arrival at Portsmouth was the reverse of departure from Calais: Alec was eventually taken from his bunk and put on a stretcher before being carried to one of many ambulances waiting on the dock. The ambulance was loaded with four stretchers, and then followed a short ride to Portsmouth Station where Alec was loaded onto a train bound for Birmingham. Like the train at Steenwerck, the train to Birmingham had passenger carriages stripped of seats; fitted with double-decker bunks and staffed by nurses. And like at Steenwerck it took ages to load the train with hundreds of wounded men. Alec's pain felt worse then when he left Calais the day before; much worse. He was concerned he was getting worse when he should have been getting better.

While the carriage was filling a nurse came to Alec. She checked his tag and a clipboard.

"Gunner Alexander Morey, 27606?" she asked.

"Yes, but you can call me Alec," he said.

"How are you?"

"My pain's getting worse. It's really bad."

The nurse frowned and she turned back Alec's blanket and checked his leg. She frowned even more. She looked at Alec. "I'll get you treated as soon as we arrive," she said.

"Is this serious?"

"This is serious and you must be treated as soon as we arrive. For now I will put you on morphine."

Throughout the long journey Alec's pain felt worse and worse despite the morphine given to him every few hours. An all-enveloping, excruciating ache that just wouldn't go away. The pain tore at him and he felt desperate to get away. Eventually the train lurched to a stop with squealing brakes. As always it took ages to get the wounded from the train, and after some time Alec was carried onto a platform beneath the largest, sooty-black glazed roof that Alec had ever seen. There he was taken to ambulances lined up in the street outside, and once the ambulance was fully loaded they commenced a long drive to the Second Birmingham War Hospital. It was a very long drive and Alec was surprised when they eventually arrived, because they were in the midst of rolling, green fields on one side, a big, brick building on the other side, and many large tents serving as additional accommodation for the injured. There were so many injured from the war; too many. Hotels were turned into hospitals, trains were converted to carry the injured, ships were dedicated to bringing the injured to England, and hospitals were overflowing with the injured. Every injured soldier had a story to tell; his own personal catastrophe.

Alec was taken into the big building where it shined, sparkled and smelt of disinfectant, as proper hospitals do. Up grand stairs and to the left into a large, open ward with simple beds lined on either side. There he saw his name and service number on a blackboard above one of those grey beds with crisp white sheets and thin grey blankets. As always the ward was strangely hushed. Alec thought about the nurse on the train, the same as when he thought about her concerns during the train journey and in the ambulance. He wondered what they would do to him. He didn't have to wait too long because two men in white coats wheeled a stretcher to his bed.

"Gunner Alexander Morey 27606?" one asked with an unusual, English accent.

"Yes, I'm Alec Morey."

"We've come to take you for your operation."

"Do you know what my operation is?"

"Amputation due to gangrene."

Alec couldn't believe he was to have another amputation. "Do you have to?" he asked.

"I'm just the porter," one man said gruffly.

They carried Alec from his bed to the stretcher and he was wheeled out of the ward and along a corridor. Alec couldn't understand what was happening. *How could they amputate a leg already amputated? What was going on? Why him? He should have listened to his father and not enlisted.* They placed Alec's stretcher at the end of a queue of three, similar stretchers. The men ahead were dealt with one after the other and then a nurse came for Alec.

"Excuse me nurse," Alec said. "Do you know what's happening to me?"

"You're suffering from gangrene so they have to amputate more of your left leg. If they don't amputate more of your leg then you will die from the poison in your system."

Alec remembered the doctor in Calais telling him about dirt and gangrene. "I understand," he said. "Do you know how much they will amputate?'

"To your thigh."

Alec was shocked by those words; he was going to lose almost all of his leg.

"I'm sorry about this," the nurse said.

"It's not your fault," Alec said automatically, while wishing it all would just go away.

FOURTEEN

For the next phase of the battle in Flanders, third division marched from Blequin to Poperinge, just inland from the beautiful and devastated city of Ypres, which the soldiers called 'wipers', probably on account of the frequent rain. The buildings of Poperinge were mostly of brick, more angular in style than Bailleul, and far removed from the attractive, French style further to the south. Poperinge was the northern Flanders equivalent of Bailleul; close to the front but far enough away not to be shelled, and bustling with British, Canadian, Australian and New Zealand soldiers. In the meantime the Australian fourth and fifth divisions had fought alongside a number of British divisions during the battles of Menin Road Ridge and Polygon Wood, which took more high ground but with the usual high number of casualties. Martin thought there had to be a better way to win the war than sending thousands upon thousands of infantrymen to slaughter.

Martin and Harry were billeted with a couple in Bruggestraat, and Martin's school day's French proved to be of no use because the area was Dutch-speaking. Major-General Monash set up his headquarters at Menin Gate in Ypres itself and Martin wasn't too keen on that. It seemed close to the front line. More of Ypres had been destroyed than left standing, and it was eerie to wander streets strewn with rubble and see the odd, part-ruined wall propped by lengths of timber to stop it totally collapsing. Perhaps one day when peace returned, those walls would be repaired and buildings reconstructed. There once was a building known as the cloth hall, apparently grand and beautiful, but all that remained was a battle-scarred tower and a few remnants of walls. Inside their new headquarters at half-ruined Menin Gate, preparations commenced for the next major battle to build upon the ground taken at the battles of Messines Ridge, Menin Road Ridge and Polygon Wood. The battle of Messines Ridge benefited from extensive planning and preparation where subsequent battles were rushed by comparison, but Martin knew that if anything was to come from the 1917 campaign in Flanders, it had to come before winter rain turned the battlefield into marsh again. On the 30th of September, the ground was dry, firm and even dusty.

The objective was Broodseinde Ridge and unfortunately Major-General Monash had limited input into the planning. Twelve divisions were to be involved, including the third, fourth and fifth Australian divisions and the New Zealand Division. As always the Australians and the New Zealanders conducted the main attack flanked by

British divisions. To support the infantry crossing no man's land, there would be a creeping barrage and machine gun fire over the advancing troop's heads and into the German lines. In the meantime the Germans had plans of their own and conducted a series of attacks at Polygon Wood, without gaining any ground.

At Headquarters in Menin Gate it was a long, wet night because rain had started at midnight, so the timing of the battle for the fourth of October wasn't a day too soon. Only things went wrong before the battle started with battalions reporting a German artillery barrage at five-thirty, just a half-hour before the Allied barrage and attack. Third division suffered casualties before the battle even started. Unlike the shock caused by the mine explosions at Messines, Broodseinde was hard fighting all the way. To make things worse Allied air superiority couldn't be exploited due to low cloud and heavy rain, although aircraft observers radioed when they saw flares launched when the various objectives were taken. Despite the poor weather and the hard fighting the ridges were taken by nine-fifteen, and Plumer telephoned headquarters to ask for feedback to continue the momentum towards the ridge at Passchendaele village. Major-General Monash thought they should but General Plumer rang back with the news that the rain and mud prevented any further advances. Artillery and ammunition were marooned because of the muddy ground and couldn't be brought up to support the infantry. Nonetheless about 1,000 yards of front was taken with third division going beyond its objectives and taking 1,900 yards, and as always Major-General Monash's obsession with training paid off well. That was at the cost of about 20,000 casualties, with about 2,000 casualties for the Third Australian Division and more than 6,000 Australian casualties.

Martin slept fitfully that night because of the dead and injured and because he knew that Haig and Plumer wanted to push on towards the ridge at Passchendaele village, despite the weather turning against such an attack. He also slept fitfully because he heard the rain on the slate roof just above where he lay in the dark.

While the men at the front were relieved for a few days, plans for the next stage proceeded and they were crazy plans too. Day after day it rained while Haig and Plummer issued edicts that 3,000 yards were to be taken in six hours, more than had ever been achieved in the dry. To the rear the guns were still positioned for the battle to take Broodseinde Ridge, and artillery drivers struggled to get their guns into place, despite planks attached to wheels to deal with the mud. Not only the guns, but drivers struggled with their horses and carts loaded with ammunition. The battle for Passchendaele Ridge was scheduled for the twelfth and it rained continuously for over a week, torrentially at times. Major-General Monash was beside himself and he pleaded with General Plumer to delay the battle in the hope that the weather would break, even just to delay for a day, but those pleas were turned down.

An artillery bombardment was supposed to be wrought in the days leading up to the battle, but it was very much subdued. Normally barrages could be heard and even felt kilometres away, but not on the 10th and 11th. There were not enough guns and ammunition in place to do the job. That bode badly for the 12th.

As always battle day started early, and given the size and scope of the attack on the ridge at Passchendaele village, the troops were scheduled to go over the top at five-twenty-five. The initial artillery barrage was weak and then nothing was heard. Major-General Monash paced the ramparts high above Menin Gate as if trying to see what was happening about two miles away. Martin sat at the switchboard with the wireless tuned to the frequency to be used by the aircraft observers, but nothing came through. He knew why.

"What's happening?" Major Wieck asked.

Martin drew a deep breath. "The runners won't be able to get through, and with this cloud our aircraft will be unable to sight the troops and their signal lamps. We're blind, sir."

"What can you do?"

There was only one thing. "I'll go forward and telephone when I get closer."

"You can't."

Martin shrugged. "There's nothing for me to do here, sir."

"Alright."

Martin exchanged his cap for a helmet, pulled on his greatcoat and went into the squalling rain. The first mile or so was easy going on good roads, but the further he went the worse it got. Duckboards crossed a sea of mud with shell craters forming little lakes all over the place. Horses had bogged in the mud attempting to get guns and ammunition into place, and were shot when they could travel no further. A small number of gunners attempted to fire their weapons while others worked at stopping their guns from sinking into the ooze on each recoil. The duckboards came to an end, shelled to pieces, and Martin took to the mud and sank half-way to his knees. He struggled onwards one step at a time and knew what the problem was. The men couldn't advance on such ground. On the right stretcher bearers carried a casualty with great difficulty, some up to their waists in mud. Martin slowed his pace, probing the ground for firmness before the next step. That way he wouldn't sink too deep. Indeed he wondered if any men had sunk much too deep, and were not shot or shelled but just trapped in the mud. Horses, carts, artillery, tanks lay scattered about; not shelled but bogged and abandoned. And for what it was worth the rain stopped. Martin pressed onwards because he said he would do so, but he wondered how he could find out what was going on. He reached the reserve trenches, kept his head low because he was tall, and pressed on along the duckboards. Closer and closer to the front trench with ladders still in place. On his right was a single soldier sitting with his back against the breastwork of the support trench while smoking a cigarette. He didn't look too good. "Can I help you?" Martin asked, getting to his knees.

"My leg...," the soldier said wincing in pain.

Martin glanced down, but the mud on the soldier's uniform hid any injuries. "I'm sure the stretcher bearers will be here soon. My name's Martin."

"I'm Jack."

"What happened out there Jack?"

"It was hopeless. We had little artillery, and the shells they fired sank into the mud without exploding. Our machine guns wouldn't work in the mud, we struggled to get through the mud, some even drowned, but the Hun pillboxes were undamaged and caused bloody slaughter. So many mates...."

"I'm sorry to hear about your mates." Martin looked around. "Can you walk if I help you?"

"I made it this far on my own so I might be able to."

Martin grabbed under Jack's muddy shoulders and lifted him, and with Jack using Martin as a support and his rifle as a crutch, they were able to return along the communication trench. "Those bloody generals...," Jack muttered.

"Don't blame all the generals Jack. There are some who didn't want this to go ahead."

"Our lot I suppose."

Martin didn't say a word. They struggled on and eventually a stretcher party approached. "Sir," one of the bearers said.

"I'm not a sir I'm Martin. You look after this man."

"We will."

Martin left them and headed out of the trench complex and west towards Ypres, to Menin gate, and there he pulled off his muddy boots and went inside in his wet socks.

"Ward!" was the exclamation.

"I'm sorry Major but it's not possible to find out what happened in a detailed way, but it's bad I'm sure. Much of our artillery couldn't get into place, and some of those which did are having difficulty firing because of the mud, while their shells sink harmlessly into the mud. Our artillery didn't damage the pillboxes and I assume much of the wire was intact. Our machine guns won't work in the mud. The mud's very thick and it slowed the troops, which would be devastating under enemy machine gun fire. Some or maybe most tanks couldn't get through. Some men drowned, sir."

"They didn't stand a chance."

"No they didn't."

"I would like to send you away to clean up."

"It's alright; the battle's not over although it is lost."

The battle wasn't totally lost, and when communications dribbled in during the afternoon, brigades were forced to retreat to within 100 yards of their starting position. The casualty numbers were not in but were expected to be very high while the New Zealanders had been slaughtered. The New Zealander Division was an excellent fighting force, and if they couldn't do it then nobody could. All in all it had been a tragic day, and Field Marshal Haig and General Plumer were to blame. It was time, well overdue, to bring all Australian divisions under Australian command and not under the British. Martin wondered if that would ever happen.

* * *

Major-General Monash stood at the graveside and read the poem in a clear, unemotional voice, belying the emotions he must have felt within. At the end of the poem, seven soldiers fired three rounds each and Major Adams was laid to rest. Four days had passed and some progress had been made, with lines pushed half-way to the objectives of the twelfth. The battle for Passchendaele came at a great cost; more than 3,000 casualties for the third division. New Zealand suffered worse with almost 4,000 killed or injured. All were due for rest, overdue for rest, and Major-General Monash insisted that third division be bussed rather than march to Blequin.

After the burial Martin went to his room and grabbed a pad. He had someone to write to and she always wrote to him too. His letter of the 16th would contain good news for a change; they would be together in three day's time. He was sure that not one of the thousands who survived the battle ever wanted to be a part of the northern Flanders section of the line again. It had been foolish to press the Germans there; the ground was unsuitable for battle except for a few short months in summer, and further south near Amiens was the only place where victory could be won. Field Marshal 'Butcher' Haig had proven himself, yet again, to be unfit for the job of commanding the British and Empire forces. Sadly he remained commander and Martin wondered what it would take before he was dismissed in favour of someone competent.

FIFTEEN

The first shell caught them by surprise and everyone ducked instinctively. The next shell landed closer with a massive, ear-shattering explosion. Alec flattened himself behind the sand-bagged wall of their above-ground trench just as another shell exploded nearby. And then the screaming started, clear and distinct above the noise of guns still firing. Alec looked across at George ripped to pieces and spread all over the dirt of Flanders.

Alec woke drenched in sweat and with his heart racing. He looked around and all was peace and calm, and he was in Ward Nine of the Second Birmingham Military Hospital. The same dream, the same nightmare, almost every night. He lay still; it was easier to lay still because it was hard to roll over with only a stump for a leg. He lay still and contemplated his situation once more, as if to reassure himself that it would be alright. But the only good thing was less pain after his second operation. His pain was manageable at least. All he had to do was hurry up and wait as Ted in the next bed would often say, or let nature take it's course as Dr Bourke always said. Eventually when his stump shrunk, he would be fitted with an artificial leg. Soon, Alec hoped, because he was bored of hospital life. Reading books, writing letters or sometimes playing cards with the men in ward nine, even though he didn't really want to play. But Alec didn't want to get his leg, get walking and get on his way home. He didn't know what he wanted: life in hospital in England or to be sent back to Melbourne. He lay in the dark and waited for the light of morning.

Slowly the ward brightened and eventually it was time for breakfast, even though Alec didn't feel hungry. He hadn't felt hungry for a month or more, and picked at his food even though it was much better than on the battlefield. Toast with poached eggs and a cup of tea with milk and sugar. After, he pushed his tray to one side and yawned with tiredness.

"Nightmares again?" Ted asked from the next bed.

Alec sighed. "Yes."

"One day you'll get over what happened."

Alec grimaced; Ted was the expert in all things. Alec didn't know what was happening to him; he was quiet by nature but over the past month or more he'd not wanted to talk with anyone. He wondered what was wrong. Why would a leg amputation stop him from feeling alive?

Dr Bourke entered the ward and stopped at each bed on the way through. Alec dreaded when his turn would come. Eventually the doctor came to Alec's bed and turned down the sheet and blankets to check Alec's left leg. He frowned and then straightened the bed clothes.

"Your leg's going well Gunner Morey," Dr Bourke said. "Soon we will fit you with an artificial limb." Dr Bourke looked at Alec. "Do you have any questions?"

Alec shrugged his shoulders and the doctor moved on.

"I'd be happy to get an artificial limb if I was you," Ted said from just across the way.

Alec grimaced, and then looked at Ted. "I don't know what I want."

"You've been feeling down for a while."

"I don't know if I'll ever be the man I once was."

"You won't be that man, but that doesn't stop you being the man you could be."

Alec knew that was true.

"You'll feel better when you get over your nightmares," Ted said.

"I suppose I will, although I don't know where they come from. They're part of what happened and not what really happened."

"The mind's a funny thing."

It was indeed.

After lunch, Nurse Walker took Alec outside in his wheelchair with a blanket over his legs, to enjoy the nice weather she said. Blue skies and a mild temperature, and Alec should have been brightened by the fresh air but he wasn't. She pushed him along a path. "I heard you have trouble sleeping," she said.

Alec knew Ted had been talking to the nurses. "I wake up with the same nightmare most nights," he said.

"I don't know what you men went through but I know it was bad. You always sleep on your back, but if you sleep on your side that might change things."

Alec thought that might work. "I'll do that tonight."

A bird chirped in one of many the trees losing their leaves and that made Alec feel better. Surprisingly better, and he was glad they went outside on a lovely, autumn day.

* * *

Alec was on guard duty with the rain beating down. His helmet and greatcoat didn't protect him from the downpour and he got wetter and wetter. He hadn't been dry for days, while his boots squelched in muddy water spilling onto the boards of their trench. About 100 yards away a crew worked in the rain sending nuisance shells to the German lines. Every 20 or 30 seconds another, dull explosion as a shell was sent across. German artillery was answering, with loud explosions from their shells landing somewhere in the distance. There was shouting and a rifle shot followed by another shot and more shouting. Alec guessed something was happening in the trenches. A flare burst high with a loud crack and lit the dark night with brilliant, white light. An answering flare burst from the enemy lines, and the scene lit by the two flares was almost ghostly, with gunners working at their 18 pounder and men tramping along duckboards in the near distance. Then another rifle shot and a shell from the enemy exploded a few hundred yards away. It was eerie, surreal; almost like a dream and yet reality.

Alec woke and recalled his dream with sharp clarity. It wasn't any specific night but any night while he was on guard. It wasn't earthly; perhaps it was hell. Perhaps he'd gone to hell and back, and perhaps there were hundreds of thousands of men trapped in hell for a moment or for the rest of their days. Alec yawned and fell asleep once more.

Alec woke the next morning clear and refreshed, and couldn't wait for their usual breakfast of toast and eggs with tea. He sat up in bed and glanced across at Ted, a Pommy driver who lost his right arm.

"Ted," Alec said. "What will you tell your family about your time on the front?"

"I don't know," Ted said. "What will you say?"

"What can we say? Even the quiet times at night are beyond anyone's understanding. After a day or a week, life on the battlefield became normal for us, but how we lived is beyond the understanding or imagination of those who haven't been there."

"You're right."

"I don't think we can say anything because they won't understand."

"I would like to say something because once this is over; we should never do anything like this again."

Alec agreed, just as the nurses wheeled the trolley with their breakfasts into the ward.

"Ted, after we eat do you want to play cards?"

"Too right. Five-hundred?"

"Yes, we'll play five-hundred."

They played 500 for most of the rest of the day, and once lights-out came at nine, Alec rolled onto his side for what he hoped would be a good night's sleep.

* * *

They sat on muddy boards surrounded by sandbags while they played a game of cards. Their rifles stood nearby, ready in case the English came. They smiled and joked, and all was normal for six soldiers in grey uniforms and grey helmets. Suddenly they heard that dreaded sound; dropped their cards and pressed close to the sandbags of their trench. The shell exploded, scattering sandbags and body parts all over. One survived with pieces of shrapnel driven into the flesh of his left leg, and he pressed himself against what was left of their sandbag shelter while all around his colleagues were blown to pieces. He turned his head and looked away.

Alec woke feeling strangely disoriented. And then he remembered his dream and wondered where it came from. Why would he remember German soldiers in a trench? And then it came back to him; his arrival at Steenwerck and the prisoners he saw. Ordinary young men looking bewildered, and that led to a dream about ordinary young men killed and mutilated by an artillery shell sent from Alec's gun. Those men were doing what they thought was right, the same as when Alec enlisted because he thought it was right. And then they were set against each other, like Alec's father said.

Alec rolled onto his back and wondered how many he killed and maimed. Too many. Too many mother's grieving for their sons, fiancees grieving for their sweethearts, widows grieving for their husbands. War was wrong.

Alec waited in the semi-dark for breakfast, and after they finished eating, Dr Bourke came into the ward and straight to Alec. He turned back the bed and checked Alec's stump and nodded approvingly. "We can fit you now," he said.

Alec nodded while the doctor called a nurse. The nurse came with a wheelchair and Alec slipped out of bed and hobbled into place. With a blanket in place he was wheeled out of the ward. He was to get an artificial leg, and soon he would join the others learning to walk again. He thought that was something at least.

SIXTEEN

Travelling by bus for several hours was far preferable to days of marching and camping overnight in tents. Even better that the officers were grouped together and their bus took them to the officer's billets of Lottinghen, Vieil-Moutier and Desvres, although it was quiet without the infantry singing songs on the way. At Desvres Martin and Harry bid their colleagues farewell and headed across the small town.

"I'll be leaving you here," Martin said quietly.

"I know." Harry paused. "Half your luck."

Martin shrugged his shoulders before crossing Place de Léon Blum and entering the restaurant and cafe.

"Bonsoir Monsieur Albert," Martin said just as he heard footsteps from the corridor. Simone came into view and raced to Martin and grabbed him so hard that he almost stumbled, given the weight of his kit on his back.

"Je suis très inquiet," she said, holding him tight.

"There's no need to be worried," Martin said in French. "I don't go to battle."

"No, your letters...."

He hugged Simone and she felt so nice. "What happened was tragic but I'm sure good will come out it."

"How?"

"We'll not make those mistakes again."

"You say 'we'."

"I'm part of it in a way, and I will do my very best."

"I know you will mon cheri."

"The weather's against major battles on any front, so now we wait until spring."

"So long!"

"I know, but one thing we can't change is the weather."

She let him go and eased away to look at him. "You're different," she said at length.

"I'm Australian."

"You don't take things seriously, unless it's time to take things seriously."

"Australians are mostly like that."

"I like it; it's nice. I like you; you're nice."

"I like you ma cherié." He took her hand. "J'aime beaucoup faire l'amour avec toi maintenant."

Simone smiled, and went with Martin up the stairs.

* * *

Martin lay on his back with his hands behind his head, and Simone curled against the side of his body with her arm across his chest.

"That terrible day I went to the front and I helped a man who'd been hurt," Martin said quietly. "One day you may see pictures of what it was like, because it's impossible to describe complete and total devastation." He turned his head and looked into Simone's beautiful eyes. "If we go on like this we'll lose this war. The British and Empire armies have been decimated, while the French army must be in disarray. I don't see a way out of where we are." Martin looked deeper into her eyes. "We wasted a quarter of a million casualties to take a few miles of ground, on top of the four-hundred thousand they lost last year on the Somme."

"If you talk about what you're going through that will help."

"Yes, I'm a lucky man. I have someone to talk with. Most don't."

"How long are you here?"

"Two weeks."

"You will feel better after two weeks."

Martin cupped her firm, fleshy bottom. "I feel better already, ma cherié."

As always they slept naked and intertwined, and as always Martin started the new day with bread and a cup of coffee. Simone went out to buy the newspaper while Martin went to the sitting room to read 'The Four Horsemen of the Apocalypse', which he bought on his last visit to Poperinge. Simone came in to read her newspaper.

"The newspaper says the war is going well and the Canadians are prepared to take victory in Flanders," Simone said.

Martin sighed. "Can I see?" he asked.

Simone handed the newspaper across and Martin read the article more or less, because he didn't read French very well. He folded the 'paper and looked at Simone. "Victory can be had for specific objectives in Flanders, but overall victory there is impossible. This newspaper's full of lies and propaganda."

"They wouldn't do such a thing."

Martin handed the 'paper back. "That article is the proof. If you want to know what war is like, you should read more than the daily newspaper," he said.

"Like what?"

"There's a good French book I heard about, Le Feu, and that will tell you what's really happening."

"I don't like complicated books. Is your book complicated?"

"It is."

"We're different." She continued reading the newspaper. The clock chimed eleven and Simone put the newspaper down. "I must get the cafe ready."

"The Australians are in town and it will be busy."

She grinned. "Yes."

The cafe was busy and Martin passed the time playing the piano with a glass of whisky on a coaster on top. At least the next day was Sunday and a day free for both of them. Simone always went to church in the morning, while Jara's stories about her tribe's version of creation caused Martin to re-think his ideas about religion, so he didn't have any, specific belief. Later they ought to get out and enjoy the peaceful countryside. It was late October and cold, but that didn't mean that they couldn't take a long walk in a part of France not rocked by artillery, where rifle shots couldn't be heard, where death and misery didn't exist. He pictured them hand-in-hand walking in silence, and enjoying that silence for what it was.

The Australians left late that evening as was their way, and given the privations of living on the line, the luxury of a meal in a cafe when billeted away would have been like heaven on earth. After Martin helped Simone and Charlotte to wash up, they went to bed late.

The next morning Martin watched Simone flicking through clothes in her wardrobe before selecting an outfit suitable for church. She laid it on the bed.

"What do you want to do today cheri?" she asked.

"I want to hold your hand and go for a walk in this peaceful countryside," Martin said.

"You would need that after what happened to you."

"I do."

"Church can wait until this evening. Come cheri; we will have breakfast and then walk to Le Mont Pelé."

After washing, dressing and breakfast; hand-in-hand they went into a cool, crisp, cloudy day. An elderly couple: he in an aged suit and top hat and she in an aged black dress, all ribbons and fancy bows, approached.

"Monsieur and Madame Leron," Simone said. "This is my friend Lieutenant Ward."

"Bonjour Monsieur et Madame," Martin said while shaking hands with them both.

"Bonjour Lieutenant," they said.

"Lieutenant Ward is here on leave," Simone said.

Monsieur Leron clasped Martin's arm. "You're fighting the good fight," he said.

Martin nodded.

After a moment they departed with 'au revoirs' all round, and Martin and Simone continued on their way. Surely they knew that Simone had a lover, and yet there was no sign of disapproval. Martin and Simone continued through the town, greeting elderly couples, married women with families and eventually they left the village behind.

"Do you want to hear my story?" Simone asked.

"Of course," Martin said.

"I'm from Boulogne. My family still lives there: my mother, my father, my older sister Laure and her family, and my younger brother Michele, although Michele is in the Armée de Terre at Aisne. My husband Gustave's family's from here, which is why we have this cafe. I met Gustave when he was working in Boulogne, but only when it was too late did I discover he wasn't the man I thought he was. When Michele came home on leave he told me about Gustave's arrest. I told Gustave's family about his arrest for mutiny, and I told them our marriage was over and they accepted that. They were good people and only he was bad."

Martin nodded and wondered what happened. Physical abuse most likely. "Does anyone else know?" Martin asked.

"Not of the mutiny, but Desvres is a small town and many know what he did," Simone said.

"What of me?" Martin asked, because Desvres was a small town.

"Gustave Belaire's not worthy to be a husband, and the Australian lieutenant is here to liberate France from the enemy."

"They will accept me even though you're married?"

"I believe so."

Martin squeezed her hand lightly and she turned her head to smile at him. "How could anyone have hurt you?" he said.

"That's over now. What of you cheri?"

"As you know I was a sailor in New Guinea, which is a British colony and a protectorate of Australia. I lived there for four yeas and I had a lover, but I had to leave her when I enlisted."

"She was from New Guinea?"

"She was."

"What of your family?"

"My parents died of cholera many years ago, and I was raised by my older sisters. I never felt an attraction to Australia, so I suppose I was searching for a home. And then I found the most beautiful place in this world."

"Your lover...?"

"She's married now."

"They marry?"

"Marriage, one man one woman, is universal."

"I didn't know."

"Underneath different coloured skins we're all the same."

They reached the lake and Simone let Martin's hand go to sit on the grassy bank. Martin sat beside her.

"Will you go back to New Guinea?" Simone asked.

Martin looked into her eyes. "For the moment I'm here with the most wonderful woman in France, but one day war will be over and I will return to my true home."

She took his hand. "I'm glad we have these moments together."

"Me too."

* * *

It was odd to be in the same hut in the grounds of Chateau Steenwerck. It seemed much longer than a year and much had changed. Major-General Monash began raids on the German lines which continued for the next few weeks. Then Haig circulated orders for urgent, defence preparations. The collapse of the Russian front had allowed the transfer of many German troops; while Martin knew the mutinies were real and almost certainly the French were in turmoil. On top of all of that, the British Prime Minister Lloyd George had lost faith with Field Marshal Haig and was considering resigning, so the allies were not in good shape for a German spring offensive. Certain for spring before the Americans had a chance to arrive in force.

In the meantime the Canadians had been ordered by Haig to continue the attack on the ridge at Passchendaele. Canadian commander Major-General Currie didn't refuse but he insisted the battlefield be prepared for battle, including building roads to bring artillery into place. While that was happening, Third division had a quiet time looking after the Ploegsteert sector. Martin spent a few days in the front lines making sure their communications lines were secure, and he was allocated a group of sappers to lay cabling deeper underground. As always the trenches were miserable, soggy places stinking of bodies left to rot in no man's land, and stinking of overflowing latrines. The Germans were fairly much engaged with the main battle but that didn't prevent them sending across nuisance shells, mostly in the late afternoons.

After the last, miserable, wet day, Martin was pleased to return to the chateau where he could hang his soaking greatcoat in their hut and warm up by the fire in the main house; a luxury after sleeping for five days in trenches. It was delightful with his back to the flames, and Major Wieck came into the parlour. Martin nodded an acknowledgement while Major Wieck came alongside and stood with his back to the lovely, crackling fire as well.

"Your job on the line...?" Major Wieck asked.

"Finished sir," Martin said. "We have our communications ready, but there'll be no more battles."

"I'm sure there won't be."

"That's just commonsense; like not trying to wade through mud up to your waist while under machine gun fire."

"You did well that day with your initiative to go to the line, and you do more than we would expect of a lieutenant. That's why I have this for you."

Major Wieck handed Martin an envelope and Martin pulled out the orders and read them, and in disbelief he read them again. "You're promoting me," he said.

"Captain Ward."

"I don't deserve this. The men on the front line deserve this; not me," Martin said while thinking about poor Jack.

"Your work has been excellent, Captain."

"In Third Division, excellence is normal."

"Take your promotion Captain Ward and good luck for the future."

Martin nodded slowly while relieved that they weren't giving him a medal. At least a promotion meant more pay and more savings for his future life. "Thank you sir," Martin said.

"Warm yourself up in here; it's much better than being on the line."

"Rain, mud and nuisance shells."

"That's right. Make sure you don't get hit by another one."

"That's down to chance or luck."

"You're right with that observation."

Major Wieck left the room and Martin contemplated the two insignias he would have to sew on his epaulets. He supposed that if he stayed at it for long enough, a promotion was inevitable. He wondered how the Canadians were doing in their quest.

Supported by their artillery the Canadians took the ridge at Passchendaele a few days later, but at a terrible cost with more than 16,000 casualties. The Germans simply retreated to previously prepared trenches further to the east to maintain their occupation of Belgium. In all the Allies lost about 250,000 men on a futile campaign in Flanders that gained a few miles of devastated, marshy ground in the middle of nowhere.

Further south the British Expeditionary Force undertook a battle to seize a German supply point at Cambrai; for the first time using a significant number of tanks, and for the first time using a surprise artillery bombardment. The British forces initially advanced some five miles with extremely modest casualties, which was impressive. Unfortunately Field Marshal Haig personally intervened and insisted that tired troops continue the offensive. The Germans were able to retake some ground and inflicted significant casualties, which was Flanders all over again. The casualties grew day by day to 40,000 men who the Allies could ill-afford to lose. Everything that Haig was involved with, even new methods of battle, turned into tragedy.

Shortly after the Canadian and Cambrai victories and the terrible casualties at both battles, third division was relieved and marching towards Blequin once more, but they didn't make it very far because they were diverted towards Armentières where the Portuguese needed relief. Once again Martin was in that hut in the grounds of Chateau Steenwerck, and he wrote a letter that he would be delayed. The division occupied the lines and Martin kept himself busy reading books belonging to Monsieur and Madame Plouvier, playing cards with Harry or playing solitaire on his own, spending time at Bailleul and just passing time. Even Major-General Monash passed time, sometimes setting off with a pad and pencils to sketch the countryside. The soldier's lot was passing time until the next, frantic battle.

* * *

Alec pulled on his artificial leg and ran the straps over his shoulders and buckled them firmly. The leg was hollow steel and almost shaped like a real leg, and it even had a joint as a mechanical knee. It worked but it took a lot of effort to walk any distance. Alec grabbed his canes and stood, and tentatively took his first steps, as he was always tentative at first. After a while he regained his confidence and was able to fall into line with the other men learning to walk again. It was bitterly cold just a week before Christmas, and not a good day to be walking around the grounds of the hospital; formerly a lunatic asylum. But Alec had to do it, and soon he was able to walk with both speed and confidence.

Alec travelled a long journey. After being fitted with an artificial leg it took a few weeks of practice before he was able to walk unaided, although that didn't make him feel better. He felt half a man, especially when he removed his leg to get into bed to sleep. Half a man and he wondered about Dorothy. She wrote that she was looking forward to his return, but Alec knew the first time she saw him one-legged, she would be horrified. It was alright to write nice things in a letter, everyone did that, but the reality would be different.

What could he do? He was a cripple and he had to pick himself up and move on. Not a man anymore, but what could he do? While he walked in a large circle following other cripples: some silent, some talking, some even cheerful, he wondered what the future would hold for him. Marriage with a woman who felt obliged to marry him, even though he could never give her what she deserved. He wondered about many things while he walked around and around the grounds of the hospital on that cold, December day.

SEVENTEEN

Simone lay with her head on Martin's chest, his heart beating fast, and he ran his fingers through her long, lush, chestnut-brown hair.

"You seem better this time cheri," she said quietly.

"It's been quiet these past few months," Martin said. "What I want more than anything else is for the Australians to be united under one commander, and then we can free France. We're commanded by an idiot dreaming about cavalry charges, and yet we have good, Australian generals who can achieve much."

"You speak harshly of your commander."

"I think war is hardening me."

"Don't become too hard." Simone sat up with her knees still astride Martin's hips. "You should be proud of your promotion, Capitane Ward."

"I am," Martin said, even though he still wasn't sure if he deserved it. But he did a good job, and his part of each battle had worked well despite sometimes difficult circumstances.

"Could you play the piano like your first day here?" Simone asked.

"Of course I will play some Chopin for you. Music to brighten the day."

"It will cheri. You can play and entertain the guests and I will help Charlotte. With the Australian officers in town it's sure to be a busy night."

"I like this restaurant," Martin said, and he meant that. "It's a place of good food, good wine and companionship, and that makes life worthwhile." He enjoyed being a part of the Restaurant Café Central every few months.

"Mon cheri, tomorrow is New Years Eve. We must celebrate together."

"We'll celebrate with champagne."

"I will make a galette des rois."

"That sounds wonderful."

"Simone climbed off and slipped out of bed. Martin rolled onto his side. "When we toast the New Year we can toast victory in 1918," he said.

Simone turned around with her eyes glistening. "I love you," she said.

"I love you too."

* * *

Alec sat in his wheelchair on the deck of HMAT Corinthe, watching the busy port of Southampton recede into the distance. Leaving England for the last time and next stop Melbourne. Travelling on a ship of wounded cripples, and that ship would, in time, return to England with a new load of volunteers to be slaughtered.

"What're you thinking of mate?" Alf asked.

Alec wondered. "We're going home," he eventually said.

"I know mate. You know it might be interesting if we hit a storm on the way. We can try our new legs while the ship's pitching and rolling."

Alec tried to picture that, and walking would be a challenge. He smiled with the vision of soldiers falling over each other in the rooms or corridors.

"Ha, I saw you smile!" Alf said.

Alec nodded. "It's taken a while but maybe it's not so bad. We survived and many didn't, and we can still walk. It's not so bad."

"It's not so bad mate," Alf said. "I signed up to save my country and win the war. Do you think we can win?"

Alec remembered the hospitals, the hospital ships, the hospital trains, the hundreds and hundreds of amputees at Birmingham learning to walk again. With so many killed and injured Alec wondered if they would run out of healthy men first. "I'm sure we'll win," Alec said.

"Then we'll be heroes."

"That's right Alf."

* * *

Life at Chateau Steenwerck proved to be surprisingly busy. Many raids were conducted with some success, especially a big raid on the tenth of February. Martin found himself involved in experiments with smoke to blind machine gunners, and later in the month there was an all-day conference for divisional commanders. They were getting ready for the German spring offensive, and as much as everyone appeared casual on the outside, on the inside they must have been worried. There were many more German troops on the Western Front while the Americans had yet to arrive in any numbers. It would take more than a few successful raids to change the course of the war, and Martin doubted that raids achieved anything more than a few casualties on both sides anyway.

* * *

Under bleak skies threatening rain, Alec looked down from his seat on the deck on the Corinthe at the two piers which made up the Port of Melbourne. He was home, but after Plymouth and Southampton the Port of Melbourne was rather small. All of the men on the Corinthe were wounded one way or the other, and many were taken off the ship in wheelchairs. Alec was determined to walk. Even though the slope of the gangway was challenging, he wanted to return home a man rather than a cripple. He waited for the crowd to abate and then hooked his kit over his shoulders, grabbed his canes and put one leg after the other, all the way to the pier decking. He waited and they came to him: Father, Mother, Ruby, Arthur, Bessie and Dorothy. They greeted each other and it seemed as if his parents didn't know what to say or do.

Arthur came to Alec and shook his hand. "Glad to see you looking so good," he said.

"I'm feeling good," Alec said, even though he wasn't. "We should catch a train."

"Let me take your bag."

Alec let Arthur take his kit and they slowly walked along the pier parallel to the railway tracks. Beyond, on the other side of Beach Street, was Port Melbourne station. The brick building with verandas could have been any railway station in England. At the station, a train of red carriages with a dirty locomotive waited. Alec wasn't able to keep up with the others and he fell back.

Ruby came alongside "How are you really?" she asked.

Alec sighed. "I wish this hadn't happened to me," he said. He thought about his situation many times during the voyage. "Three men I served with were killed by shells, so in a way I was lucky. Some will come back unharmed except for what they went through, and some won't come back at all. I have this and I have my memories."

242

"If you ever want to talk about your memories...."

Alec looked hard at his beloved sister. "I don't know if I can. It was like those paintings or operas which try to depict hell, only it was real and I lived through it. At the time it seemed perfectly normal, and only later when I was in England did I realise what it's like."

"I know you wrote to us many times and I will keep those letters always, but will we win?"

Alec was careful about what he wrote; knowing his letters were read and censored. "I don't know," he said. He remembered their discussion one night in a cafe about tens or hundreds of thousands of casualties to take a few miles. "Don't tell anyone but I don't think we can win."

Dorothy took his arm. "You did what you had to do and I'm proud of you for that," she said. "Things will be as they once were."

They reached the station and all occupied a compartment of varnished wood and green leather seats. A few minutes later the train whistle blew and they jerked into motion. Soon they were rocking and rolling past small, brick houses and terraces on either side of the railway line. They could have been any house or terrace in England. Alec gazed out of the window at a middle-aged husband and wife heading towards a shop on the corner, and it was as if the slaughter on the other side of the world didn't even exist.

That couple would never know what it was like. Reports and casualty lists in the newspapers couldn't possibly portray the madness and the futility.

"What are your plans?" Father asked.

"I'm still serving although on leave," Alec said. "It will be some time until I'm discharged."

"All jobs were taken while you were away, but you have a trade and I'll do what I can when you're ready to work."

"Thank you Father."

"Can you work?" his Mother asked.

"Of course Mother," Alec said. "I can work and we can get married as we planned. There are many like me, perhaps thousands during the time I was in hospital, and all of those men will get on with their lives."

The train crossed the dirty, brown Yarra River and pulled up at Flinders Street station, which was quiet and empty after what Alec experienced in England. Alec saw many fit men and especially men his age, and those men wouldn't understand and could never understand. They used the subway to go to Flinders Street to catch a tram home. Walking the last few hundred yards from the tram stop in Mount Alexander Road, and Victoria Street hadn't changed at all. It seemed eerie and dream-like to be there, as if no time had passed and 100 years had passed. They went inside the little, timber house to the sitting room and Alec was relieved to sit and relax in one of the armchairs, but not in his uniform. But he didn't want to go and change, so he sat with his artificial leg hidden beneath coarse khaki. They all took chairs: Father in the other floral-coloured armchair, and Mother, Dorothy, Ruby, Albert and Bessie squashed on the floral-coloured couch. The room hadn't changed, with a clock and many trinkets on the mantel above the fire, and a painting of rural England on the opposite wall.

"I kept cuttings of the articles of your time at the front," his mother said.

Alec was surprised. "Thank you Mother," he said.

"I can get them."

"There's no need."

"It's no trouble."

She got up and was gone for a moment before returning with a hard-backed book. Alec turned over the pages and glanced at the first article, but what really interested him was the 20th of September 1917, the day before his injury. He flicked the pages and then reached that date. 'The Germans had fortified their positions and withdrawn their main line to the eastern edge of the plateau which ran from Zonnebeke and the roads towards Menin. It was the Northern troops and the Australians who carried these positions, advancing to a depth of 1,500 yards and taking Veldhoek and the western edge of Polygone Wood - the principal centre of German resistance. Further north Zonnebeke was captured and the London Territorials supported by the Highlanders, captured a second line of farms. The next day the Germans, in their costly and unsuccessful attempts to retake the lost positions, suffered exceedingly heavy losses without gaining any ground.' Alec frowned. It was like reading the description of a card game rather than war where thousands were injured or killed, where medics dealt with casualties and doctors dealt with worse casualties, where towns were half-destroyed and farms were nothing more than churned over earth and shell craters. The newspaper article was strange and surreal and not like anything.

"What do you think?" his mother asked.

"It's good Mother," Alec said while thinking he could never explain the reality because nobody could. Nobody could ever explain and nobody could ever understand, unless they were there.

Ruby got up as did Arthur. "We must go," she said. She bent down and kissed Alec's cheek. "Goodbye brother," she said.

Arthur shook Alec's hand. "Good luck for the future," he said.

"I must go too," Bessie said. She kissed Alec as well. "Goodbye brother."

They left.

"Do you want to stay for dinner?" Mother asked Dorothy.

"If it's no trouble," Dorothy said.

"Of course it's no trouble!"

"Thank you."

Mother left for the kitchen, leaving Alec alone with Father and Dorothy.

"You look good," Dorothy said to Alec.

"Thank you Dorothy," Alec said. "I'm glad we're together again." Alec wanted to say more but didn't know what to say. He doubted he would ever be able to say what he truly felt. They waited in silence while Mother cooked chops in the kitchen.

"I should help your mother," Dorothy said, and she left the room.

Alec glanced at his father who never wanted him to go to war. He wanted to say something but couldn't. There was a wall between them which Alec knew could never be crossed; not then and not ever. They sat in silence except for the clock on the mantel ticking. Alec was relieved when Mother came to the door and asked them to go to the dining room. For a brief moment he wished he was at the front where life was simple and uncomplicated; firing artillery shells until a shell got you. Alec sighed. He wondered if life could ever be normal for him. He doubted it.

"Do you want my help?" his father asked.

Alec wondered, but the time would come sooner or later. "Yes Father," Alec said.

"Take my arm and we'll see what they've cooked for us."

Alec took his father's arm so they could go to the big, round table where chops, green beans, mashed potatoes and a cup of tea waited. Alec wished he was far away from there, but he didn't know where. Just anywhere but there. But there was nowhere to go, so he had to be helped to the table to eat his chops and drink his tea as if everything was normal. He looked at Dorothy smiling at him and smiled back as best he could. A fake smile was something at least.

* * *

Towards the end of the first week of March, Third Division AIF was marching south to their usual rest billets near Bléquin and Martin was curious. Simone wrote that she had something important to tell him but he couldn't imagine what it was. He hoped she didn't plan to divorce her husband for him, because although he liked her he didn't love her. Then he wondered if she could divorce her husband anyway. Whatever it was she wanted to tell him face to face.

"A penny for your thoughts," Harry said.

"Pardon?" Martin asked. "Oh, I got a strange letter from Simone a while ago, and I asked her to clarify something but she wouldn't. I don't know what it is."

"We'll be there soon enough."

"Pity they didn't take us there by bus.

"That only happens if you've been massacred."

"I'm glad we're marching."

"Me too. This will be our last for a while. This might be our last for a long while."

"I know mate. Where do you think?" Martin asked.

"Not Flanders."

"Only an idiot would attempt to win the war in the mud of Flanders."

"You know that Haig still thinks there's a place for cavalry on a battlefield?"

Martin nodded his head. "I can picture his cavalry charging amongst tanks and dodging strafing by aircraft."

"Why haven't they sacked him?" Harry asked.

"I think they would dismiss him and we can only guess why they haven't. They have a coalition government in Britain and that may make it harder to get agreement for his dismissal. Possibly there's no-one better."

"Their generals went to the same schools, were trained the same way and fought in the same battles."

"That's possible."

"Amiens," Harry said. "The Huns will push to take Amiens and then Paris."

"You're right mate," Martin agreed. Maybe they would never see Flanders again.

Third division camped that night near Lembres, and after a nondescript breakfast of hard biscuits soaked in a mug of tea to make them barely edible, they packed their kits and started the last day's march to Bléquin where the majority were billeted at a number of farms, mostly in barns and tents, while the officers continued to Lottinghen, Vieil-Moutier and Desvres; each about half an hour further on. At Desvres Martin went to Restaurant Café Central and used his key to let himself in. All was quiet except for the steady ticking of the clock upstairs. Then Martin heard creaking on the stairs and Simone slowly came into view.

"Bonjour cherié," Martin said.

"Bonjour cheri," Simone replied. "Je suis enceinte," she said.

"Pardon?" Martin asked, confused.

"Enceinte," Simone repeated while placing Martin's hand over her stomach.

Martin was shocked. "I didn't understand," he said in French. I really speak English."

"It's two months. Are you happy?"

"Of course I'm happy," he said while digesting the news. "We're going to have a child together."

"What does that mean for you?"

"We must marry."

"Do you love me?"

"Of course I love you," Martin said automatically.

"What is love?"

"Heart to heart, mind to mind and body to body. What's love to you?"

"A good man who loves me and who takes care of me."

Martin digested that. "You know that I love you."

"I know."

"I love you Simone," Martin said, while knowing there was something missing and always had been. But they got on well together and he hoped that was enough. "Will you marry me?"

"Of course, after I divorce my husband. We should make plans."

"You're giving birth in seven months time and I'm caught up in this war."

"Plans about when the war is over and when we can go to New Guinea."

Martin's heart sank and that was over for him. "New Guinea's quite rough and not a place to raise our child."

Simone looked upset with her lower lip almost trembling, and Martin really felt sorry for her. "I have you and that's much more important than going to New Guinea," he said.

"We can go to Australia," Simone said hopefully.

Martin didn't want that either. "I left Australia to go to New Guinea."

"Where?"

"Here. If I'm still in the army when your time comes, what will you do?"

"Go to my parents in Boulogne."

"You go to your parents, and when I'm finished with the army we'll start a life together."

"Yes we will do that," Simone said.

That wasn't what Martin wanted, but Simone was a nice woman who he liked a lot, and he was sure that they would have a good life together. "I love you," he said.

"I love you too," she said.

Martin kissed Simone's cheek and hoped that things would work out. With his hand still on her stomach he was surprised that he barely felt anything. "Our baby is very small," he said.

"It is early days."

"Can we make love?"

"Of course, but I would prefer to talk. Let's go to the kitchen."

Over a delightful cup of coffee in the cosy kitchen warmed by the range, Martin repeated his letters about the upcoming German spring offensive, and how the war could be lost after the terrible casualties at Flanders. They held hands and talked for a while, and then Simone prepared the cafe for lunch and later for dinner. At the end of a long day they went to bed, Martin still without a nightshirt and not wanting to sleep in his underwear. They didn't make love but just sharing that bed felt nice.

Martin drifted into life at his home away from home and eventually they made love, although he sensed a distance between them and wondered what it was. They made love a few times over the next few weeks, and always at the end Simone pulled on a nightgown, kissed Martin's cheek and rolled onto her side to sleep. Their happy abandon of sleeping together naked was over.

Martin was startled by heavy knocking early one morning; a morning after they made love the night before. Simone pulled on a robe before going downstairs. He heard Harry trying to tell her something, which was quite impossible because she spoke little English. Martin pulled on his underwear and went to find out what was going on.

"Mate," Harry said. "It's started."

"What's started?" Martin asked before realising. "The offensive?"

"Yeah mate. Tomorrow we're heading to Ypres."

"Bloody hell, Ypres!"

"I know."

"What time are we leaving?"

"From the square at five to pick up the rest at six."

"Right mate."

"I'll see you tomorrow."

"See you mate."

Harry left and Simone turned to face Martin. "Tu devez aller?"

"Oui," Martin said. "Demain matin."

She took his hands. "Be careful."

Martin put a hand on her stomach. "We have to win this war for us and for our child."

"I'm sure you will win."

Martin hoped they would win.

EIGHTEEN

They marched north-east for three days before being intercepted by messengers with orders to proceed to Steenwerck to catch trains to Mondicourt, just north of Amiens. It took a further day to head south-east, arriving at the railhead on Monday the 25th of March. Apparently Major-General Monash had been on leave and was returning, while the GSOs were doing their best to sort out where the 20,000 men of third division were to go and, more importantly, how they were to get there. Train after train pulled out, and after an overnight journey, they arrived into a tiny French village surrounded by chaos, with British troops, trucks, cars and carts fleeing the advancing Germans and choking the roads. Choking was an understatement and it was amazing that anything was able to move along the arrow-straight roads that bisected the plains of Picardie. As the trains rolled in one after the other, third division was gradually sorted into order brigade by brigade. In the meantime Major-General Monash found a chateau in Couturelle, which didn't last long because they were ordered to report to Corbie. Major-General Monash used two cars to transport as many as he could, but given the chaos on the roads they didn't reach their destination until past midnight.

Monash then met with the British and was issued with orders to join the British Fourth Army under General Rawlinson, and take a line between Méricourt l'Abbé and Sailly-le-Sec. In the meantime third division were taking a line 20 miles to the north, and everyone worked all night to arrange busses to take third division to their new lines, which were trenches from one of the previous battles in the area.

The British continued to flee in great numbers which was ominous. At daybreak on the 28th, Martin went with Major-General Monash to a chateau on high ground near Franvillers, where they saw advancing German cavalry, advance German troops and even German armoured cars forcing back British cavalry. The line was open and undefended and it was critical that the Australians get into place to prevent the enemy taking Amiens. Fortunately the first busses arrived, and despite two days with no sleep the Australians briskly and efficiently marched east to take their lines, and Amiens and perhaps France had been saved. The British rout continued but that didn't matter anymore.

Marshal Foch took overall command of the operation which showed that the British government had lost faith with Field Marshal Haig, and Foch ordered General Rawlinson to advance towards Morlancourt. The battle was conducted by third division, but with no artillery support, and communications between headquarters and the front net yet tested, the advance failed; fortunately without too many casualties. They were unable to take the village of Sailly-Laurette and the advance dug-in some distance short of their objective. With artillery in place and communications fully established, there was more success on the 30th. Unfortunately the Germans were able to take the town of Le Hamel from the British further to the north, and the resulting bulge in the front line exposed Allied troops to enemy fire and enabled the Germans to overlook Allied rear areas. Then the Germans launched an offensive against Villers-Bretonneux on the fourth of April, which was repulsed by a combined Australian and British force.

The chateau at Franvillers came under German artillery fire and third division headquarters was forced to relocate to the chateau of Comte deThielloye at St Gratien. Bad news came in; at Flanders the British had lost Messines Ridge, Armentières and Ploegsteert Wood. The Australian First Division was sent to Flanders to save the day, while the second through fifth divisions remained on the Somme, with a joint headquarters at Chateau de Bertangles near Amiens. A massive sandstone building of three storeys and attic rooms; surrounded by overgrown lawns and entered from a long, gravel driveway. More than big enough to be headquarters for four divisions of the Australia Corps. By then the German advances ceased and stalemate returned to the Somme. Later in the month on the 24th, the Germans launched an assault on Villers-Bretonneux with four divisions and several tanks, and took the town which gave them the ability to shell the city of Amiens. Fortunately Villers-Bretonneux was re-taken by the Australian Fifth Division that night, and handed over to the residents on the morning of the 25th of April.

Then third division was sent away for rest in Amiens, which was a city close to the front like Bailleul and Poperinge, only much larger. Beautiful French architecture, a particularly magnificent and imposing cathedral, many shops, much industry and even a tram service. One part of Amiens was ancient, perhaps medieval, where small and plain buildings crowded narrow streets. That was a poor area with many women dressed in old, shabby clothing and many children running about in little more than rags, and often in bare feet. The city had been shelled and there were a number of damaged buildings, but fortunately the majority of the thriving and bustling city was intact. Martin was billeted with Monsieur and Madame Dellacourt, their young son Albert and their daughter Sophie in their lovely, two-storey home about two miles from the city centre. He spent a few days taking in the sights and especially the cathedral, although sections of the exterior and interior were protected by sandbags and the stained glass windows and the interior fittings were removed. The cathedral was the largest Martin had ever seen, much more imposing than Notre Dame in Paris, and particularly light and spacious inside with a towering ceiling seeming to reach towards the heavens. Like the rest of third division, all Martin could do was tour the sights and write to his fiancee who would, at least, receive his letter a few days later. Simone replied that she read so much about the success of the Australians and how they saved France. While Martin re-read her letter he wondered if all they had in common was a war fought by one to save the country of the other, and that war would come to an end one day. He hoped that wasn't the case.

* * *

Martin dealt the cards for the next hand when Major Wieck burst into the room carrying a manila folder. Martin paused and looked up at the major.

"When you've finished your game you'll be interested in this," Major Wieck said.

Martin reached for the folder and inside was the plan for the Battle of Hamel from the new commander of the Australian Corps, General Monash, as sent to the new commander of third division, Major-General Gellibrand. It was thick, typical for John Monash, and very detailed. Le Hamel was a small town nestling beneath higher ground, where German artillery had a good view towards any approaching forces. Martin frowned while he read the plan, and on battle day minus fourteen there would be barrages of gas and smoke shells at three each morning. Martin pondered that and realised that it was a plan of surprise, and the two weeks of barrages were to condition the enemy to expect gas on the day of the battle. The next stage was to bring 46 machine gun crews into position by battle day minus one, but only moving at night. Sixty of the latest model tanks were to take part, as well as four supply tanks to carry ammunition and other supplies as the advance progressed, doing away with the need for hundreds of horses and carts. The battle tanks were to wear the colours of the battalions they were supporting, which was an excellent way to avoid confusion. Eighteen bombing aircraft were included as well as a number of older model aircraft to mask the noise of the tanks being brought up to the start line. Communications were by runners and telephone as well as signal lamps from the front lines to aircraft observers, as first used at Messines, carrier pigeons, portable wireless sets and rockets to send messages to headquarters. Martin doubted that rockets were a practical proposition; they would end up anywhere and everywhere, but the rest was sound.

On the night before battle the Australian wire would be cut and the tanks would move forward, their noise masked by aircraft flying above the lines, at three the barrage of smoke shells would commence and the Germans would pull on their gas masks, as always hampering visibility and movement. At three-ten the main barrage would commence, aircraft would bomb trenches and the Australians would advance with the enemy totally unprepared. As the advance proceeded, both the supply tanks and bombing aircraft would bring supplies to the troops, the latter by using parachutes. At the same time a diversionary attack was to be undertaken on Ville-sur-Ancre to the north. The second, third and fourth divisions would provide five brigades augmented by ten companies of American infantry under the command of Australians. General Monash estimated the village and the trenches beyond would be taken in 90 minutes on the fourth of July, 1918.

Martin put down the plan and thought it a masterpiece, the smartest yet, building upon the success of Messines and using the latest technology: tanks, bombing aircraft and portable wireless sets. "This plan's amazing," Martin said, and he meant it. He knew what John Monash was capable of when given free reign, and he was sure the 90 minutes would prove to be correct.

Then would follow consolidation, the usual enemy counter-offensive and establishing permanent supply lines and communications. But with the village and the line won what followed was modest by comparison. He couldn't wait for the day of battle to see how it played out. If it played out well then it would be the beginning of a new type of warfare which could only lead to Allied victory.

"What is it?" Harry asked and Martin gave him the plan. Harry frowned while he read it and Martin wondered why Haig would give John Monash, a colonial, free reign. The British looked down on Australians as inferior colonials, and they particularly looked on Australian soldiers who they thought were undisciplined. And then it dawned on him. Harry put the plan on the table and looked at Martin. "This could work," Harry said.

"This could win the war," Martin said.

"It could."

"They're running out of men, and now it's time to try something different. They need Australia to show them the way."

"They wasted the last of their conscripts in the mud of Flanders."

"They did."

NINETEEN

Pre-dawn on the eighth of August, just over a month after the great victory at Hamel, and all waited for a much bigger battle written to the same script. Led by the Australian Corps and the Canadian Corps and supported by the British and the French, a surprise battle was to be conducted with no preliminary artillery bombardment, and using tanks and aircraft. The attack started not with hundreds of yards of ground taken but miles of ground taken, more than two miles in three hours. The advance continued so that by the end of the day, the Canadians had taken more than eight miles, the Australians just under seven miles, the French five miles and the British two miles. At the rear, tens of thousands of German prisoners were being dealt with.

The advance slowed somewhat the following day. Infantry had outreached artillery support, supply lines were stretched, communication was difficult and many tanks were out of commission. Despite that the Allies advanced 12 miles into formerly German-held territory. On the 11th, having outrun artillery support and supply lines, the battle of Amiens paused while artillery and supplies were brought into place.

The next day Martin borrowed a truck and a driver to visit divisional headquarters at Chateau de Bertangles. Martin climbed on board and greeted Mick who was typically, laconically Australian: stretched out relaxed and smoking a cigarette.

"Where to Martin?" Mick asked.

"Rue du Chateau; just off Route Nationale north of Amiens," Martin said.

Mick ground the gears roughly and they were on their way, heading east across the plains of northern France.

"I never thought I'd see the day...," Mick said.

"I didn't either," Martin said. "That's why we're going to divisional HQ. General Monash's going to be knighted."

"Get away!"

"It's true. The King's coming to knight General Monash."

"I didn't know they did that."

"It's been many, long years since a commander was knighted in the field. You can form part of the honour guard."

"I'd like that. By the way, how's things with you?"

"Easier than it used to be," Martin said. "I used to lay out miles of telephone cables and connect up switchboards, but there's no need for that now. Advancing miles rather than yards mean we would never keep up, so we communicate by wireless instead."

"That would be easier."

"It is."

After twenty minutes driving they turned off Route Nationale and followed the left and right turns to reach the chateau; an imposing sandstone building at the end of a long, gravel drive surrounded by trees and immaculately groomed grass. There was much activity as several drivers assembled a display of captured German artillery and trench mortars. That wasn't Martin's job and he didn't belong with divisional headquarters staff either, but the knighting was something he wanted to see. John Monash had achieved much during the past six weeks and he fully deserved his honour to come. Major-General Gellibrand and the other divisional commanders were on the steps of the chateau, and beyond were about 600 drivers and infantry lined in four rows along the gravel drive. Two cars, one a black Rolls Royce, drove into the grounds and stopped part-way along the drive. A number of officers and the King in uniform got out. The King inspected the near rag-tag honour guard and then the captured trophies before a stool was placed at the top of the steps of the chateau. The King spoke briefly with the commanders before General Monash knelt to be dubbed on his right shoulder, and then the General went to rise and the dubbing of his left shoulder was rather hurried with a few laughs from the honour guard...

After pinning a medal and putting a sash around General Monash's neck, the King and his party departed for their cars. As they got in General Monash shouted 'three cheers for the King!' Not too many cheered, they were Australians after all, and Monash shouted 'come on!'. The honour guard tried again but it was little better, and after barely an hour it was all over. Martin sought out Mick and they headed to their truck for the drive to their newly-relocated divisional headquarters at Chateau de Franvillers.

Martin's role in a newly mobile war had changed significantly, and of course he was working for a new commander. Major-General Gellibrand once had military training in England and he had experience going back to the Boer War, but he didn't have the insightfulness of John Monash. Indeed he argued a lot with General Monash but was always overruled. Monash always appreciated hearing other points of view, and sometimes he would have reasons for doing things certain ways and other times he would change his plans. Gellibrand wasn't like that. He was far from that.

The next battle was scheduled for the 21st at the ruined town of Albert to take the Albert to Arras railway, for a combined force of British, Americans and the Australian

Third Division, and planned by General Byng. Like the Battles of Hamel and Amiens, preparation was undertaken in secrecy with units brought up to the line at night, artillery concealed as far as possible, and the battle would feature bombing aircraft, tanks and wireless communication to the troops on the ground. On a densely foggy morning at four fifty-five, the troops advanced protected by a creeping barrage, and supported by tanks and aircraft. With the element of total surprise initial advances were made to the north, but fighting was heavier in the south, where the Americans and British bogged down in what had become a hot, summer's day. Fighting continued the next day until General Byng paused the offensive to allow forces to re-group. New plans were issued for the 23rd which included an additional French force, and that allowed the town to be taken and the battlefront continued to advance on a fifty-mile front towards the next major town: the ruins of Bapaume. Further south, General Monash had the Australian Second Division taking Mont Saint-Quentin which was no easy task given the Germans held the high ground and the Australians were significantly outnumbered.

The Germans had fortified Bapaume and General Byng was tasked with planning the battle, with the lead to be taken by the New Zealand Division assisted by the Australian Third Division. The forces surrounded the town on the 28th, and after heavy fighting amidst houses and rubble, the Germans were forced further east on the 29th. Two days later the Australian Second Division captured Mont Saint-Quentin; General Monash ordered his men on the right to 'scream like bushrangers' to distract the enemy from the main frontal assault, and that was followed by Australians working in small groups to separate and disorientate the enemy. Martin knew that John Monash could achieve victory against the odds through his detailed plans, and more importantly by making sure each and every man under his command knew exactly what he must do. After taking Mont Saint-Quentin, Monash and the second division forced the enemy out of Péronne, and the Germans fell back to their Hindenburg Line on the Canal de Saint-Quentin.

* * *

Alec looked at his uniform in his wardrobe and never wanted to wear it again. He was discharged being medically unfit with a disability due to active service.

"Alec," his mother called. "Dorothy's here."

Alec shut the wardrobe door, grabbed his sticks and walked along the corridor to the sitting room. There he went to a chair and flopped into it awkwardly. "Hello Dorothy," he said.

She bent down and kissed his cheek. "Hello Alec," she said. "How are you?"

"I'm better now that the army has discharged me," Alec said truthfully.

"Now we can make plans," Dorothy said.

Plans to get married, of course. "I have to get a job first, and then we can save for a deposit on a house."

Dorothy sat on the arm of his chair and held him. "I don't think I can wait that long for us to be married."

Alec understood, and it had been a long time.

"We could marry and move in with my parents." Dorothy said.

Alec thought that was a good idea, but there was a better one. "When Father retires next year, Allens said they would give me a job in his place, and then we can marry and live here."

"Would your parents let you?"

"There's plenty of room, and we can help them with expenses while we save for our house."

"That's good for both of us, and good for your parents.

"Yes it is," Alec said, even if he wasn't sure if marriage was good or not.

"Have you read the latest 'papers?"

Alec nodded slowly and thoughtfully. He barely believed what he'd read the past few months, weeks and even days. "How did they do it?" he asked.

"You were there."

"I was and it was terrible. Many died and many more were injured, and yet in the past months we're winning the war. Australia's winning the war."

"Australia and Canada."

"That's right. How did they do it?" Alec asked, more in wonder than anything else.

"After four years they must have changed things."

Alec had read about some of the changes, like tanks, surprise artillery barrages and aircraft bombing enemy trenches. He wondered why they didn't do those changes earlier.

"You should be proud that you played your part," Dorothy said.

"I'm just glad to be home," Alec said, while not sure if he really wanted to be home or even get married.

Dorothy squeezed his hand lightly. "We'll marry when you get a job, and then we'll buy a nice house when we can. The future will be good for us both."

Alec hoped it would be.

* * *

At the headquarters for third division at, disturbing news dribbled in. Apparently the fifty-ninth battalion of the Australian Fifth Division initially refused to abandon a rest break in order to return to the line, but were eventually persuaded to do so. A week later the first battalion of the Australian First Division was ordered to the front shortly after relief and refused, and 119 men temporarily deserted. Those were mutinies of admittedly exhausted soldiers, and fortunately small-scale and isolated incidents. Martin wondered how they would play out because under Australian law, if found guilty of mutiny, the men involved could be shot. He doubted that would happen because shooting soldiers wasn't the Australian way.

The assault against the Canal de Saint-Quentin and the well-fortified Hindenburg Line was planned by General Monash. It was on open ground typical of Picardie but had a number of ridges to cross, with the canal passing through a four mile tunnel. That was an obvious place for the Allies to advance and it was well-defended by the Germans. Given there was no possible element of surprise, the battle plan was more traditional with a massive, preliminary bombardment in the days before the attack, and a creeping barrage to support the advance. More tanks were brought up, and once again American troops were put under Australian Command. Two American divisions, the twenty-seventh and the thirtieth, were to initiate the battle on the 27th of September by clearing German forces from outposts in front of the line. Unfortunately they did so poorly, so those objectives were rolled into the main attack of the 29th.

Amidst fog and rain, the American Twenty-seventh Division was tasked with taking the northern end of the tunnel and the American Thirtieth Division the south, with the Australian third and fifth divisions to go ahead and take the Hindenburg Line. The American Twenty-seventh Division was unable to penetrate and the Australian Third Division had to take objectives originally assigned to Americans, by which time most of the tanks were out of the battle due to German artillery fire. Following on from the American Thirtieth Division, the Australian Fifth Division further to the south was able to make more progress. With third division bogged down over the tunnel, Australian reserve brigades were sent in. But American communications had broken down and nobody knew where they were, which meant artillery couldn't be used to support the battle for the risk of shelling the Yanks. Martin overheard an argument down the phone between Gellibrand and Monash and tried to keep out of his COs line of sight.

"Ward!" Gellibrand bellowed. "Why aren't the Americans communicating?"

"They have wireless sets, signal lamps, runners and flares for when they take their objectives," Martin said.

"They couldn't take an objective if their lives depended on it. Do they know what to do?"

"They were trained and they have signals officers like me."

"What are you doing about this?"

"I rang the RFC and they put on extra flights, and they will ring me as soon as their observers see something. Although with cloud, smoke and rain, it will be difficult to sight troops on the ground."

"I have to send in our troops without artillery cover."

"We're reliant on the Americans, sir."

"Tell me as soon as you hear something."

"Yes sir."

In the midst of that problem, the British Forty-sixth Division crossed the canal over the Riqueval Bridge and took thousands of prisoners before proceeding towards the Hindenburg Line.

The battle for the tunnel over Canal de Saint-Quentin petered out at nightfall before resuming the next day with good progress by the Australian third and fifth divisions, finally taking the first trenches of the Hindenburg Line later that day, and clearing the second line of trenches the following day. The third and fifth Australian divisions were then given orders to proceed to Amiens for rest, with General Monash visiting Chateau de Franvillers in person to congratulate everyone involved.

* * *

Martin sat on the steps of the chateau and stared off into the distance across the peaceful plains of northern France. Harry sat beside and handed an envelope across.

"Thanks mate," Martin said.

"What're thinking of?" Harry asked.

"We nearly lost this battle because of a breakdown in communications. It was almost a catastrophe and too many men died."

"I was glad that was you and not me."

"We'll win this war in less than a hundred days."

"We will."

"It makes you wonder." Martin had thought about their recent progress many times over the past weeks. "John Monash has achieved so much these past few months, and I wonder if the British had done things differently, we wouldn't have suffered as many casualties. Then I think we wouldn't have won so easily if Haig hadn't worn down the numbers of German soldiers over the years."

"He attempted to win the war with battles of attrition, thinking the Allies had more men then the Germans. Only he lost so many men that he nearly lost the war."

"That's right," Martin agreed. "When Haig eventually tried new strategies like at Cambrai with tanks and a surprise bombardment, he didn't plan the battle in enough detail, and then he made a last-minute change which resulted in tragedy; two things that John Monash would never do."

"And Passchendaele...."

"That was idiotic."

"Passchendaele and Cambrai followed by the defeats in March seem to have been the last straw, and the British allowed Foch to command Haig."

"Yes they did." Martin opened the letter from Simone and read it. He put it down. "Simone's closed the cafe and has gone to stay with her parents. She's also reading about how the Australians are saving France."

"What are you going to do together?"

"I like the cafe and I would like to do something like that. They rented that cafe, but I have money invested in Australia and I could put a substantial deposit on that cafe or one similar. With my capital and Simone's expertise it'll work out for us."

"I'm sure it will."

"What are you doing mate?"

"I'm twenty-six tomorrow, and soon I'll be home and marrying my fiancee."

"Happy birthday for tomorrow."

"Thanks mate. The rumour's they're negotiating an armistice."

"I know."

TWENTY

Alec heard the bashing and crashing and his mother went outside to find out what was up. But he knew what it was after one false start: the war was finally over and the street was noisily celebrating with rubbish bin lids. Mother came inside.

"It's happened at last," she said.

Alec was relieved. "An armistice?" he asked.

"Yes, from eleven this morning in Europe."

"The eleventh of the eleventh."

Alec was glad the war was over, and a war like that must never happen again. He hoped that everyone had learned their lesson from a catastrophe that rocked the world for four, long years.

* * *

Martin stared out of the window across Place de Léon Blum: grey and miserable with steady light rain swirling. On the other side of the world, paradise was warm with the sun beating down from a cloudless sky. Handsome men and beautiful, bare-breasted women went about their chores, while happy, naked children laughed and played without a care in the world. He sighed and turned around to survey the restaurant, with the only sound being the clock ticking upstairs. He had his home, the restaurant with living quarters upstairs, a mortgage, a fiancee and a baby daughter Annette. He smiled briefly about another Annette, real name Marie. He wondered how she fared.

He opened the piano stool and took out the scores before sitting and arranging them in place. He hit the opening hard and that brought back memories. Hard all the way through like he always played it, and then he heard crying. Simone came down the stairs.

"You woke the baby," she said.

"I'm sorry," Martin said. "I'll play softly."

Simone went away and Martin had a fiancee who sometimes scolded him, and a baby who slept lightly. He played the softer scherzo and even softer largo before stopping. The louder final movement could wait for some other time.

"You should be marching in Paris today," Simone said.

Martin turned to look at her. "My khaki uniform's the wrong colour against French blue."

"You Australians won the war."

"Australia had a small force but we contributed more than you would expect from our size, especially with battle tactics. But we were only a small force and never capable of denting a big power like Germany."

"You won in the end though."

Martin knew that Australian strategy, and Australian and Canadian soldiers taking the lead in the final offensives won the war. "In the end we won," he said.

"How do you feel about your role?"

"I kept communication open between commanders and troops; and communication was as essential as any other part of a battle. One day near the end we had two American divisions assigned to us, and one failed to communicate even though they could have sent runners or used their signal lamps. I think they froze under fire. We sent Australians in, but we couldn't use artillery to protect them because we didn't know where the Americans were and we could have shelled them. That cost many hundreds of casualties, and could have lost the battle."

"You served well." Simone said.

"But that's over now and we have the rest of our lives together." A cafe in Desvres which was a pleasant village of friendly people, and not far from Simone's family in Boulogne-sur-Mer. Simone's husband Gustave had signed papers for their divorce from his jail cell, Martin purchased the cafe from the landlord, and soon they would get married in front of a magistrate. Martin wanted two children and Simone promised to be more careful for the future, although Martin sometimes wondered if that accident was really an accident. Never mind, what was done was done, and there was no use dwelling on what might have been. "We'll be fine cherié," he said.

"I know we will."

Martin knew they would be fine.

EPILOGUE

Total casualties for the Great War were 37 million, with 17 million deaths and 20 million wounded. There were 10 million military deaths and 7 million civilian deaths. The Allies had 6 million military deaths and the Central Powers had 4 million. Of the military deaths, about 2 million died from disease.

Australia from a population of 5 million had about 60,000 deaths and 152,000 wounded. That was a casualty rate of 65% of men who embarked for service; the highest casualty rate of the Allies and reflecting the aggressive, front-line roles that Australian forces were often assigned.

The Great War officially ended on the twenty-eighth of June 1919 with the signing of the Treaty of Versailles. That treaty confiscated 10% of Germany's territory won from previous conflicts, but still left Germany the largest and richest nation in central Europe. Germany was left largely unoccupied except for a strip along the Rhineland. Financial reparations were linked to Germany's ability to pay and went mostly unenforced. Germany's military was restricted in size while Germany and her allies had to take full responsibility for causing all the loss and damage during the war. That clause was unpopular in Germany at the time.

Germany's post-war economic problems stemmed from a shattered economy caused by the war effort, government corruption, economic incompetence and a world-wide depression from 1929 onwards. Unfortunately the German public's perception was that Germany's post-war economic problems came from the Treaty of Versailles, and that perception sowed the seeds for future conflict.

Alec and Dorothy married on January the tenth, 1920. They had their first son Alexander Sundell later that year. Later they borrowed to buy a house in Oakleigh where it was an easy, flat walk to the nearby railway station, which was important for Alec. At Oakleigh they had non-identical twins Ronald Lillie and Keith Alfred; my father. Alexander Lillie Morey died on the twelfth of December 1949 of peripheral circulatory failure related to the injuries he received on the battlefields of Flanders in 1917. He was 52 years old.

The battles which brought an end to more than four years of trench warfare became known as the 100 days offensive, even though the actual time to victory was 95 days.